Damsel
NOT

KRISTINA CIRCELLI

Copyright © 2014 by Kristina Circelli
Cover by Sarah Ashley Jones / Cover Photo by Dawn Pendleton
Editing by Juli's Elite Editing
Formatting by JT Formatting

http://www.circelli.info

Circelli, Kristina
Damsel Not/Kristina Circelli – 1st ed

Library of Congress Cataloging-in-Publication Data
ISBN-13: 978-0-9763728-8-2
First Edition: September 2014

1.   Damsel Not - Fiction 2.   Fiction - Romance
3.   Fiction - Contemporary

For Dawn, Jordan, and Amy
My Very Favorite Bad-Ass Maidens

Chapter 1

SHE STARED AT THE WHITE-TIPPED crests of the morning ocean, crystal-blue eyes scanning the churning swells that matched the anger in her heart. For too long she watched the Pacific sea rage, hearing only the rush of wind past her ears, feeling only the aching loneliness of being that single, solitary figure on the long stretch of sand.

Soon the beach would fill with bodies, families out for the day, couples stretched out alongside one another. Some would be alone, out for morning jogs or taking time for themselves to read a good book. But they would be alone by choice.

She was not.

"You left me," she whispered to the sea, hands clutching a vase against her chest, eyes misting despite the fury building in her chest. The sky, filled with the lightest touches of reds and oranges, blurred before her. "You promised to stay forever. You're a liar."

Silence greeted her words, said with such venom that her jaw clenched together as soon as they passed her lips. She wanted to be furious, wanted to hate. It was so much easier being angry.

You can't think like that. You have to be fair, remember all the good things.

Her best friend's words came back to her, spoken so softly to the wounded woman hiding in the back room of a house that had lost its warmth.

It's okay to be angry, but you have to let yourself mourn, too.

She'd turned away from her lifelong friend then, pushed aside the only person who knew all the right things to say, even if she wouldn't listen to them at the time. She fled the house filled with people all there to celebrate a life ended too soon and escaped to the beach – the place they met, the place they married.

She'd known him for nearly all of her adult life, loved him almost as long as she'd known him. Everyone said they'd been an odd pair, the wild-child writer and the straight-laced accountant, but they made their differences work as best they could. Neither ever considered themselves romantics and so they often found themselves at arm's length, but their love was never questioned, never faltered.

But now that love was gone, one-sided, and she was left missing all their imperfections, all the things that made them so wonderful.

Yes, it was so much easier to be angry.

For three months she'd tucked herself away from the rest of the world, refusing to speak to friends or family, barely working, hardly eating. Instead she spent her days battling the fury in her head and the despair in her heart. Nightmares plagued her, memories of what once was, shadowed forebodings of an empty future. And, yet, the hint of something promising awaited her, something she wasn't ready for – and she hated herself for daring to believe she would ever laugh again. She never remembered her dreams when she awoke, just the feelings that came with them.

"Sometimes I feel like I did on our first date," she told the waves, stepping into the water and letting the cold sea wash past her ankles. Fear crept into her with every inch the water touched. Wild child she'd always been, but the ocean and everything it contained scared the hell out of her. But she had to do this, for him.

"I think about that day a lot. When you teased me for being afraid of sea monsters, and threatened to throw me in the ocean. I was so mad at your teasing, but kind of thrilled by the thought of you picking me up and throwing me into the water. You never did, but the idea of it was enough for me."

Farther she walked into the ocean until it touched her calves. A shiver worked its way up her back. "Sometimes I feel like I would after we had a fight. So annoyed with you, but also laughing to myself about how stupid we could be."

The sea washed against her knees, which were nearly trembling. "Sometimes I feel lost, the most painful emptiness. You remember how I used to feel so lonely for no reason, like something was missing that I couldn't identify? It's all I feel now."

Her thighs chilled at the touch of the water as a wave washed against her, but she stopped there. She wouldn't, couldn't, go farther than this. "Sometimes I feel hopeful, like there is something that's supposed to happen and I'm going to be happy again. And then I get so mad all over

3

again, because why should I be happy when I couldn't save you?"

She shook her head, hating what she was about to do, hating that she wasn't strong enough to do it sooner.

"We promised each other that we wouldn't be stuck in the ground for eternity. We promised to free each other in the sea, so our spirits could travel the world forever. I'm sorry it took me so long to fulfill that promise, but I just ... I wasn't ready to say good-bye."

Her fingers trembled as she uncapped the vase, hands shaking as she tipped it, jaw clenching against the sorrow that invaded her senses as the ashes poured into the ocean, spreading around her in a halo of memories. She swallowed hard, reaching out and touching a finger to the water, watching her late husband's ashes ripple away from her.

And so, in the canopy of color that brought forth a gorgeous dawn, she said good-bye. Good-bye to the only man she'd ever loved. Good-bye to the life they'd built together. Good-bye to the anger that was blackening her heart.

With the loss of that anger came the first tears she'd cried since the day he left this world for the next, and, for the first time, she let herself mourn.

2

Eight Months Later

"ISABELLA DAWN NEVEAR! YOU HAVE fifteen minutes to get ready or I'm dragging your ass out of this house in your sweats!"

Disturbed from a fitful sleep by the chirpy voice of one Olivia Candor, Izz managed to throw a pillow in her friend's direction. "Get out."

Olivia only chuckled and threw the pillow back. "Come on, girl. We're going out."

"I don't go out on weekdays."

"Good thing it's Saturday then, huh?" She raised a brow when Izz opened one eye and glared across the room. "Come on. You, me, and the girls are going out. You need some socialization." Olivia stalked over to the closet and began rifling through her friend's collection. When they were younger, they'd both been known to sport some wild styles, and even though their tastes had matured some, she was pleased to see some of the old outfits still hung next to the conservative blouses and skirts.

"Here."

Izz lifted herself to her elbows, her face framed by thick and messy blonde hair. When she stood, those golden locks would fall mid-back, but, for now, were contained in a loose braid. Her almond-shaped blue eyes took in the clothing at the foot of the bed. "I haven't worn that in about ten years."

Olivia scoffed and avoided the second pillow Izz threw at her. "Well, you still got the body for it, so no bitching. Now, get up and take a shower. You smell."

Izz fell back down and pulled the comforter to her chin, rolling over onto her stomach and facing the other direction. "Don't want to. Go the hell away."

With a huff, Olivia stomped over and stripped the blanket from the bed, saying a silent prayer of thanks that her friend was clothed. "Girl, you are almost thirty years old. Don't make me bathe you like some mother hen. Now get your ass up. Fifteen minutes!"

With that final command, Olivia tossed back her shoulder-length black hair and stalked out of the room, hoping Izz would follow direction. Once, in another life, they would have both leapt at the opportunity to enjoy a night on the town, getting all dolled up and causing chaos wherever they went. Polar opposites in appearance – Izz with long golden tresses that were never styled and Olivia with dark hair always kept in tightly bound curls, Izz with the body she worked hard to keep toned and Olivia happily round in all the right places – the friends since childhood shared a common passion for adventure.

Olivia missed that part of her best friend. Izz had been tamed some during her years of marriage, to the point that Olivia used to wonder if she was truly happy, though there had been the edge they all loved about her. But since her husband's death, Izz had retreated inside herself, living within the worlds she created for millions of people for entertainment rather than face the reality just outside her front door.

Tonight, that would change.

As she waited for her friend to shower and dress, Olivia perused the living room. She'd been in that room hundreds of times, but loved it a little more with each visit. Her friend had eclectic tastes, from the beautiful antique chair in the corner to the world's ugliest metal chicken statue by the couch to the ancient-looking sword hanging above the fireplace. She stopped at the sword, tracing a finger down the smooth, cold metal.

"How many fucking times have I told you not to touch the sword?"

Olivia jumped at the sound of Izz's harshly spoken question, then let out a whistle when she turned and saw her friend all dressed up. Izz wore a form-fitting black dress that fell mid-thigh and dipped low down her back, showing off the edges of a tattoo. On her feet were black heels that gave another inch to her 5'6" frame. She wore minimal makeup and her hair was still wet, but Olivia knew that once it dried it would somehow manage to form into long waves that she was forever jealous of. "Damn, girl. You clean up nice."

"Whatever. You wanna go, then let's go."

Izz stalked past her friend, who was also dressed to kill in a dark-red skirt and skimpy black top, weaving around messes she hadn't bothered to clean over the last few months. Unable to stop herself, she adjusted the sword, which had been knocked off-center by her friend. Her fingers gently touched the edges, moving the sword back to its proper place.

"Shit," Izz muttered when the blade bit, slicing into her thumb. Blood pooled along the lesion, already streaked on the metal. "I've had this thing my whole damn life and it's never cut me."

"Well, that's what swords do, babe. They cut," Olivia put in wryly, handing her friend a handful of tissues.

Izz accepted them with a smirk, first wrapping her thumb then using the last tissue to wipe the blade. Focusing on the sword, she allowed her eyes to travel up its length, to the hilt. A dragon crest was carved into the blade just where it met the hilt, the dragon's appearance mimicking the tail that formed as the metal curved up and around the wielder's hand, ending in a point. The gold metal glinted beneath the lights, reflecting greens and blues that looked like scales. In the center of the hilt was an oval-shaped indentation. Izz guessed that once, long ago, there had been a stone in the spot to complete the grand look of elegance the sword radiated.

When she turned away from the metal, a flash of light, along with the slightest hint of a face, caught her eye, causing her to jump and take a second glance. Her own distorted reflection peered back at her.

"What's up?"

Shaken from her thoughts, Izz shook her head. "Nothing. I thought I saw something. Let's go."

NIGHT WAS UPON THEM BY the time they reached the beach bar hangout, the moon high in the sky and the stars outshined by the lights of the city. Izz let her friend lead her through the packed parking lot and into the bar. She barely saw the crowd, didn't feel herself brushing against anyone as they passed, only showing signs of being alert when they finally came to a stop at a booth in the back.

Time to put on the happy face, she managed to think before that booth came to life with the sounds of squeals and laughter.

Four women poured out of the booth, wrapping Izz in hugs. She hated hugs, despised being touched, but allowed them this one moment since it had been months since they'd seen her. While she waited for them to finish their greeting, cursing them out in her mind, Izz gave them each onceover.

There was Deanna, tall and willowy, with a killer smile and attitude that would put even the hardest of men to shame.

There was Miley, short and stout, with a mass of uncontrollable red hair and the loudest voice Izz had ever heard.

Then there were the twins, Beth and Jackie, who looked as identical as they behaved, nearly comically so.

She loved these girls, as different and similar as they all were, and, she realized when they finished their hugs with giggled apologies, she'd missed them. All five of them had been there for her when her husband passed, even when she pushed them away, and here they all were now.

"It's not a party without Izz," she said with a forced grin, using the line they'd all uttered many times in the past.

Miley slid an arm around her friend's waist, laughing when Izz shoved her away with a scowl. "Then let's get this party started!" Her voice rang out across the bar, attracting the attention of everyone in their vicinity and bringing forth a round of laughter as the six women slid into the booth, Olivia taking a chair at the end.

It was hard, being around them again, despite how much she missed them. They'd gotten into a lot of trouble over the years, had many memories of crazy nights and even crazier mornings. Once, it had been nothing for them to end up at a party two states over or sign up for a last-minute bungee jumping excursion. Izz craved adventure, and that passion fueled her career.

Her husband had hated that reckless side of her, sometimes scolding her like a child for her tendency to put herself in harm's way ... especially the times when harm's way resulted in a broken bone or nasty bruise. In time, she'd come to see he was right, that she was an adult and must play the part, no matter the burning desire in her heart that told her she was meant to do bigger and better things, to explore and leave the world churning in her wake. Where those feelings came from, she'd never quite understood, but, in time, she learned to suppress them.

When a round of shots was placed on their table, courtesy of a group of men a few booths over, Izz reconsidered her life the past nine years.

What the hell, she figured, picking up a shotglass and toasting to her friends. *Time to be a little reckless*.

Chapter
3

THREE ROUNDS LATER, ALL SIX women were on the beach, gathered around the bonfire that always signified live music night at the bar. Joined by the men a few booths over, they danced to the sounds of indie rock and laughed at one another's uncoordinated moves.

Everyone except Izz. She stood close to the bonfire, feeling the effects of the alcohol. Typically she didn't drink in public, knowing the risks of doing so, but right now she enjoyed the way it dulled her emotions and made the night that much more tolerable. Her earlier resolve had dimmed, rapidly replacing recklessness with boredom. So much boredom, in fact, that she turned her back to the fire and her dancing friends and walked away, into the night, needing a few minutes alone on the beach.

When she was far enough away that the music was only a dull roar, Izz stopped, wrapping her arms around herself to ward off the chill. The wind carried Miley's raucous laugh to her ears, causing her to let out an amused breath. "Some things never change," she said to herself.

"Talking to yourself, lass?"

Startled, Izz dropped her arms and spun around. She

resisted a sigh when she saw Breckan Bex standing not three feet from her, and was surprised she hadn't heard his approach. Normally, she was far more observant. Yet another reason why she didn't particularly enjoy drinking. It threw off her senses.

"Hey, Bex."

"Haven't seen you in a while. Been missing you." He took a step closer, a soft smile on his handsome face, a smile accented by the lilt in his voice that had most women weak in the knees.

Izz wasn't one of those women. There was something about Bex that creeped her out, and she'd never understood why her late husband kept the guy around as a friend. Bex had wormed his way into their lives nearly ten years ago when he took over a branch of the office, and she'd thought of him as a plague ever since. He looked good enough, with short-cropped brown hair that managed to be both messy and styled, and grayish-green eyes that always held a twinkle of mischief. Girls flocked to his sturdy physique and charming grin, but Izz saw through it all. What exactly she saw instead, she could never quite place, but the guy had been on her shit list from day one.

"I've been around," she answered casually, turning in the direction of the bar. "I should get back."

"Hold on." He grabbed her arm when she passed, pulling her closer to him. "I was hoping we could chat for a bit."

Izz glanced down at his hand, back at him. "Take your hand off me, Bex. Now," she ordered when he didn't move.

"Maybe we could go out for dinner," he suggested in that foreign Irish tongue of his, ignoring her request. "I admit I've always been intrigued by you, but by the time I found you, you were already taken. Maybe now–"

"Maybe now you can take your goddamn hand off me before I kick you in the throat," she finished for him, her voice laced with the promise of her threat. "I'm not interested." Anger mixed with panic when she yanked against his grip, only to have his fingers tighten. A quick glance up at his face showed a surprisingly earnest expression that was betrayed only by the annoyance in his eyes.

Breckan Bex wasn't used to women turning him down.

"Bex. I won't tell you again."

"One dinner, and you'll change your mind about me," the man replied.

"You have three more seconds to get the fuck away from me." Izz began counting in her head.

"Ah, come on, my dear Isabella, you know you've always wanted–"

"Three."

In one swift movement, Izz pulled her arm back and spun. She intended to punch the sleaze in the jaw as hard as she could, but as soon as she was free something took over her body, a force of deadly and absolute control she hadn't felt for years, directing each movement until her leg was extended and her foot connected with the man's neck.

Bex fell to the sand, gasping for air, as Izz stopped her spin and righted herself with perfect balance. Before she could even see Bex, her mind was racing with the truth of what just happened. It had been a long time since she'd trained with her father, who'd insisted that she learn the art of self-defense from the time she could walk. But in all her years, she'd never actually had a chance to practice those skills on an attacker.

She couldn't remember the last time she'd moved so fast and with such precision, let alone lifted her leg high enough to actually kick a man taller than her in the throat. The past few years of her life had been about control, not letting go of it just because someone annoyed her.

What the hell just happened? she asked herself, backing away from Bex. The man was letting out strangled gasps, but started to get to his knees. Brushing off her shock for the moment, Izz raced back to the bar and found Olivia, who was getting up close and personal with one of the bouncers.

"Go, we have to go," she ordered, and the edge in her tone had Olivia agreeing without a moment's hesitation. Izz didn't wait around to say her good-byes and marched out to the car, knowing her friend would catch up.

"What's going on?" Olivia asked when they got in the car and pulled out of the lot. "What happened when you left?"

Izz took in a deep breath, not sure if she was ready to go back into that moment. Part of her wondered why she was so upset. After all, Bex had come after her, refused to let her go. Surely he deserved it. But, at the same time, she'd attacked one of her late husband's best friends. Wild and reckless she may have once been, but never was she that aggressive. Apparently she'd graduated from grieving to depressed to just plain violent.

"I want to get out of here."

"Relax, girl. We're going home."

"No." Izz shook her head, hands clutching one another. "Out of this town. Out of this state. Away from this whole goddamn coast. Now."

Olivia looked over at her friend, worried about the look on Izz's face. "I'll see what I can do."

FOR THREE DAYS IZZ PACED the halls of her empty home, terrified Bex would show up wanting revenge, confused by how she'd managed to evade him, desperate for an escape. Olivia kept her updated on travel plans, ordering her to be at the airport at 7 AM Wednesday morning with enough clothing to last her a week. She wouldn't tell where they were going, but Izz didn't care.

As long as she was away from this house and these memories, she would go.

After what had to be her tenth pass through the living room, Izz came to a stop in front of the sword that hung on the brick wall. She'd avoided it since that night, convinced she'd seen a face in the flash of light that shone after her blood was spilt by its edge. Her thumb throbbed as she approached, though she supposed that was her own mind's doing.

The metal was clean, blood and smudge free, a perfectly ordinary sword in most ways. In its full length, the sword rose to just above her hips, most of it sharp metal until it met the gold hilt. A more untrained eye wouldn't see the intricacies in that metal: the smoothed edges, the shallow etchings, the slightest indentations made for a man's fingers. Her father had passed the sword on to her for her thirteenth birthday. It hung in their family home until she moved into a house of her own, when it came with her.

"Keep it safe, keep it near," her father had told her on that fateful birthday. *"This sword has been in our family*

for generation upon generation. It was given to me by my father, and now I pass it on to you."

"Why?" a younger Izz had asked, not yet appreciative of things that held such weight. *"Who gave it to our family?"*

Her father had only smiled and touched a hand to her head. *"No one knows for sure, Isabella. While we know many stories of the world, that one was lost over the years, but, one day, perhaps in your time, it will be retold."*

And so she kept the sword, cherished it as a gift from her father. It would be the last gift he would give, as he passed away before her fourteenth birthday, alongside her mother in a car accident that left two adults dead and one child orphaned. Izz lived with her grandmother, a fierce and mean-spirited woman, until the day she turned eighteen, the day she packed up everything she owned in the trunk of a beat-up Mustang and hit the coast with Olivia. Never once did she look back, except to remember her parents, and her old life, fondly.

Once she'd tried to research the origin of the sword as a way to remember her father, but all searches came up frustratingly empty. Now it hung as mere decoration, though, she had to admit, she had been known to remove it from its mount and attempt a few practice swings. Both her mother and father enjoyed sparring, either with swords or in the boxing ring, and that passion had rubbed off on their only child.

Feeling that calling now, Izz reached up and grasped the hilt, careful not to touch the blade again. The weight of the sword was familiar when she pulled it from the wall and held it before her – nearly too heavy to lift, the handle a bit clunky in her palm. The sword wasn't forged for her, but for a wielder long since passed.

But that didn't matter. Ignoring the imperfect fit, Izz entered into a dance only she knew, the blade glinting beneath the lights with each flick of her wrist, twist of her arm. She jabbed and parried, spun and stepped, every movement as fluid as the blood that pumped through her veins. Her body remembered this dance of woman and sword; her mind remembered the images of knights and maidens her mother used to daydream about; her soul remembered the feeling of home that came with the touch of the weapon.

"Son of a bitch," she muttered as she stopped midstep, feeling a mix of emotions that tore at her: wonder over childhood memories returning to her, sadness for the loss of everything she'd ever loved, excitement that, even after all these years, she still found comfort in pieces of her past.

"You're losing it, girl," she said to herself, shaking her head to rid the thoughts. Her eyes traveled down to the sword. "As for you, you can just stop with the nostalgia. Real life doesn't allow for trips down memory lane."

With a huff, Izz set the sword back on its mount and stalked into her bedroom to finish packing, then locked up the house and left for the airport. She didn't spare the weapon a second glance, nor did she allow herself to remember the memories staring back at her retreating form.

Chapter
4.

"SO YOU FINALLY GONNA TELL me where we're going?" Izz asked when she met Olivia at the airport.

"You finally gonna tell me what brought on the sudden need to get away?" Olivia asked in return. When Izz merely lifted a brow, she crossed her arms. "Then I guess you get to wait. Come on, the girls are already inside."

"The girls?" Izz repeated. "How did everyone get a week off on such short notice?"

Olivia laughed. "Please. Trust-fund-baby Miley hasn't worked a day in her life and never will. Beth had some vacation time saved up. Me, Deanna, and Jackie are bringing our work with us." She nodded at a large bag over her shoulder. Olivia and Jackie worked as event planners, Deanna as a manager at a temp staffing agency. "And we all know you can work wherever you want."

She wasn't wrong. Izz readjusted her own work bag on her shoulder and followed her friend into the airport, meeting up with the girls and breezing through security after Olivia gathered their tickets. Izz let herself be led through the motions, barely registering anything said to her, not really caring where they went so long as it was away from the west coast.

Izz settled back in the small plane seat, casting a look out the window, pleased Olivia had secured her a window seat. It wasn't until the pilot's voice came over the intercom and announced their destination that she turned back to her friend, who was sitting next to her.

"Myrtle Beach?" she asked, repeating the pilot's statement. "Why Myrtle Beach?"

"Why not?" Olivia replied with a shrug. Then she grinned. "Plus my parents have a timeshare there, so it was super cheap."

"Works for me." Izz sat back and returned her stare out the window, her thoughts drifting back to the sword, and her sanity.

JACKIE TOOK CARE OF THE rental car when they arrived in South Carolina while the others grabbed their bags from baggage claim. An hour later they all piled into the SUV and began the drive to the beach.

"You'll love this place, Izz," Olivia said from the passenger seat, where she was playing the part of navigator. "We'll have to double up on the beds, but there is plenty of space to just hang out. Plus it's right on the water."

Izz kept her gaze out the window as they drove, seeing signs of a season in full swing. Groups of tourists milled about, wandering in and out of shops, dining in the fresh air. They looked happy, and she narrated the scenes in her mind, sketching them for the future when she would return to this moment in her memories.

Finally the ocean came into view, the opposite coast

from the one she'd been born and bred on. Izz hadn't spent much, if any, time on the east coast, and was looking forward to exploring what the other side of the country had to offer. She watched the waves, remembering the last time she'd been in the water, when she watched her love's ashes float away with the tides.

Stop. She shook her head, trying to rid herself of any negative thoughts.

"Home sweet home," Olivia announced as Jackie pulled the SUV into a parking garage attached to a towering building. "For the next week, anyway."

Once they were out of the car and filed into the lobby, Izz glanced up at the sign, which read *Southern Suites.* Olivia checked them in and led everyone up to the tenth floor. Inside the room, they all took a moment to explore. It was a small but well-stocked timeshare, with a full kitchen and cozy living room decorated with a nautical theme. A large couch lined one wall with a driftwood table in front of it, and an oversized recliner sat in the corner. A flat-screen TV was across from the couch, resting atop a small shelf. Three lamps shaped like shells were at either end of the couch and next to the recliner.

A large bathroom was just off the living room, with an adjoining bedroom that held two beds. The second bedroom was a little bigger, with just one bed and its own bathroom, and a separate entrance to the narrow balcony, which overlooked the Atlantic Ocean.

"Not bad, Liv," Izz complimented, dropping her things in the master bedroom and claiming it for herself and Olivia.

"What can I say, I do good work." She grinned, then clapped her hands together. "Okay, so, I say we order some pizzas and take the night to chill. Tomorrow, we're hitting the beach."

THE NEXT DAY THEY DID just that, all six women hitting the shore in the morning with books, magazines, and work in tow. Beth, Miley, and Jackie immediately went for a walk, while Izz stretched out on a towel between Olivia and Deanna, lying on her stomach. Her intention was to nap despite the relatively early hour, but a low whistle from Deanna had her opening her eyes.

"My, my, gals, look at that fine specimen."

The three turned their attention to a man in his early twenties jogging past them. He was attractive by any definition, but Izz only rolled her eyes. "Don't you have a new man back home, Deanna?"

"Hey, I'm allowed to look," her friend protested with a laugh. "Besides, he's just a fling."

Izz closed her eyes again, not interested in further discussion of men. Jackie and Beth were happily married, Deanna divorced but on the prowl, Miley a jumper of relationships, and Olivia happily single. That left Izz, the widow not sure where she stood in the grand scheme of relationship seeking.

"What do you think, Izz? Red board shorts over there or hottie with the ribs tat?"

Cracking one eye, Izz glanced in the direction Olivia pointed, seeing two men tossing a football. One was sandy haired and tall, the other a couple inches shorter with dark hair to match the black ink on his torso. "They're both fine, I guess."

"But which one is hotter?"

She knew what Olivia was doing, and allowed herself to fall for the bait. "The one with the tat."

"I knew it!" Triumphant, Olivia sent a grin over at Deanna. "Always was one for the bad boys."

"So they say."

"Can I ask you something, Izz?" Deanna gave her friend a side glance. "You always went for the wild types growing up. Then you settled down with a straight lace. You think you'd still go for straight lace now?"

"Or come on back to the wild side," Olivia put in with a wicked grin.

Izz lifted a shoulder, resting an arm beneath her head. "Does it really matter?"

"Of course it does."

With a sigh, Izz pushed herself up and peered over at her friend. "I don't know, okay? I don't even want to think about it. Yeah, I always went for the wild guys. They were fun and kept me on my toes. But Eric … he made everything feel safe and stable and, I don't know. Like there was a future outside of just having fun." She sighed again and shook her head. "That doesn't even make sense, I know."

"Sure it does," Olivia replied, almost reaching out to touch her friend on the shoulder before remembering the 'Don't touch Izz' rule. "You feel what you feel. If you want to go safe, then go safe. If you want a night of reckless, wild fun with a guy whose name you won't remember in the morning, then have at it." She grinned again when Izz merely lifted a brow. "You do you, girl. Move forward. Live."

With her friend's words echoing in her thoughts, Izz rolled over and stared at the ocean. Deanna wasn't wrong. She did always prefer the wild guys, then ended up with one who would rather build a computer than mountain bike down a nature trail. But that was love – it struck in strange places sometimes.

Even with that love still in her heart, Izz couldn't deny the desire in her heart to do something stupid every now and then. Get in a swordfight, bungee jump off a bridge, enjoy a long weekend with a guy she just met in some lodge deep in the woods … things she'd been known to do in the past.

Maybe it was time to move forward, she decided. Rediscover herself, or at least some part of the girl she used to be. Living in grief wasn't fun. It wasn't living.

And, she realized with a small smile, she was ready to live.

Chapter 5

IZZ WOKE UP EARLY THE next morning, alone in the living room. She preferred sleeping on the couch the past few months, not quite used to the feel of an empty bed. Even though she would be sharing with Olivia during the trip, it was still the couch that called to her, room enough for a single person.

Taking advantage of the quiet, Izz powered up her laptop and opened a new document. For a few minutes, she just sat and stared at the blank page, feeling over-whelmed with the thought of starting writing. Her deadline was approaching, and, while she'd never missed one, part of her didn't really care. Work was just another thing get-ting in the way of living right now, when in the past it had been the one thing she truly lived for.

But she needed the escape now, that adventure into new worlds crafted by her own mind, where anything was possible if she could only dream it so. Slowly her hands lowered to the keyboard, mind already racing with possi-bilities. A woman in mourning. A world where villains ruled. An ages-old battle between good and evil. Magic, love, adventure.

This was her return to self.

Lost in the creation of her own mind, Izz set to work, tuning out everything around her – the sound of the ocean, the chill of the air-conditioner, the feel of the uncomfortable couch. For right now, all that existed was this computer, and the words appearing on the screen. A couple hours passed before signs of life appeared in the condo, though she did her best to drown them out.

"So, Izz. What do you prefer? Knights, gladiators, or wizards? Izz? *Izz!*"

Startled, Izz jumped, so absorbed in her work she hadn't heard the question, which, judging by her friend's irritated expression, had been asked several times. After Olivia repeated herself with a huff, she frowned. "Uh, why?"

"Just answer the question."

Repeating the three options, she knew it was an easy choice. Wizards were cool and all, and gladiators were pretty bad ass, but knights were definitely her type. "Knights," she answered, turning her attention back to the computer and not seeing the grin that crept across her friend's face.

"SO THIS IS WHY YOU wanted to know," Izz said to her friends the next night, staring up at the enormous building. *Not even a building*, she thought. A goddamn castle. A thick stone wall created a square more than an acre wide, with a drawbridge at its center, which was currently lowered on two enormous chains to allow people across a moat. An actual moat, with actual fish and plants. Turrets rose at each corner of the castle, adorned with flags of different colors and crests. Cutouts in the stone created windows, allowing light in and out, which likely accounted for some of the vegetation growing along the sides of the walls.

When they drew nearer, Izz saw the name of the place scrawled across above the drawbridge in swirling letters: *Quest for Avalon.* "Seriously?"

Miley laughed and linked her arm through Izz's. "Yes, seriously! This is going to be a blast."

"They have different shows depending on the day of the week, and the season," Olivia explained as they walked up the cobblestone path. "You choose knights, so we choose Friday."

"You guys are ridiculous," Izz muttered, letting Miley drag her up the walk and through the massive entryway, which was on the other side of the drawbridge. Flags of all colors surrounded the front walk, stamped with insignias of nations she was sure would come to light during whatever show she had been roped into seeing.

Once inside the castle walls, Izz had to admit she was impressed. Whoever owned this place had gone all out, creating a marketplace along one side reminiscent of medieval shops with vendors decked out in regalia selling all types of wares, from souvenirs to swords. On the other side were podiums with old battle gear proudly displayed. As they walked farther in, Izz saw an entire city bustling about, with food carts set up in corners, tables strategically placed to see the street performers, and actors playing the roles of villager, merchant, and even soldier. It was all a little overwhelming, Izz managed to think as she glanced around, trying to take everything in but knowing she would need an entire day to truly see and appreciate all the intricate details.

Finally they reached the back of the square, where a large wooden door barred their sight from whatever lay just beyond. With a wide grin, Miley yanked the door open and pulled Izz inside. Just inside the door the six paused, letting their eyes adjust to the dim lighting. A narrow passageway urged them forward, lined with metal sconces flickering firelight above their heads. The shadows were a mix of eerie and intriguing, and, despite herself, Izz felt excitement overcoming irritation the farther they walked.

Finally, the passageway opened up into a large gathering room, lined on one side by a bar and the other an elaborate seating area. Behind the bar were women dressed in colorful linens that clung to their tiny waists and flared out at the hip, their hair pulled back in braids and accented with flowers of all types. The drinks were served in wide-rimmed mugs, so authentic looking that Izz knew they must have cost a pretty penny each.

But the place spared no expense, she realized the more she looked around. This one room was more elaborate than any place she'd ever seen before, with the smallest of pictures carved into wooden walls and the grandest of statues depicting knights at war.

"Come on." Olivia interrupted Izz's visual exploration by taking hold of her friend's wrist and all but dragging her into a separate room.

"Where are we going?"

"Pictures with the king, duh." At Izz's blank stare, Olivia burst into laughter. "Okay, so we splurged. We all wanted to give you an awesome night out, so we bought the Knight's Bounty package, which is like all-out, full-on experience. Special pictures, unlimited drinks, front row seat, special dessert just for us. You name it, we got it."

She was about to protest, not happy they spent what she was sure was a hell of a lot of money on her, but Deanna shushed her with a firm yet friendly glare. So instead she relented and let them drag her into the picture room.

"Good evening, m'lady," a man standing just inside the doorway greeted with a grand sweep of his arm. Beck and Jackie returned the greeting with an exaggerated curtsey, giggling, while Izz rolled her eyes.

So cheesy, she thought, but had to smile at her friends' behavior. They, all of them, had always been quick to play the part of wherever they were. One of her favorite trips with the girls had ended with them pretending to be pirates aboard a cruise ship. They may have been pushing thirty, but sometimes it was fun to just be a kid again.

"The king awaits," the man said, taking position behind a camera sitting atop a tripod. A woman, whom Izz assumed to be his assistant, placed small halos of silk flowers atop their heads and sashes across their shoulders. "For the beautiful women of the court," the man said as his assistant led them to a small platform, where stood another man.

Izz had missed him when they first walked in, more concerned with laughing to herself over the cameraman's cheesy accent and vernacular. She took a quick moment to observe the "king" – a man of average height decked out in a flowing red cape, a tunic of sorts covered with elaborate stitchings depicting a battle scene, and thick trousers tucked into black boots that laced almost up to his knees. He was, perhaps, in his mid-forties, thick beard covering a

handsome face – what she could see of it. His eyes crinkled at the corners as they stepped up to him.

"Six beautiful women at my side," he said in the same
accent as the cameraman. "To what do I owe this honor,
m'ladies?"

Miley smiled so wide Izz thought her cheeks would
break. "The honor is all ours, good sir."

Izz scoffed to herself, not surprised to see Miley,
Beth, and Jackie completely enraptured with the handsome
king. They'd always been suckers for hot guys with even
hotter accents.

After the picture, Izz followed the girls back to the
main room and over to the bar. A drink of some sort was
pressed into her hands.

"Courtesy of the Knight's Bounty pass," Olivia told
her with a wink. "Drink up."

She wasn't interested in getting drunk tonight, but
took a sip of the fruity beverage to appease her friend and
was pleasantly surprised to find it was non-alcoholic. They
wandered the room for a bit while they waited for the
show to start, purchasing a few souvenirs and filling up
their mugs. Miley opted for a frozen strawberry blend
while Deanna went for a local brew.

"What's she up to?" Izz asked Deanna when she
caught sight of Olivia leaning against a podium of sorts,
chatting with a man wearing a headset.

Deanna followed her gaze, then shrugged. "Probably
giving him our names. Supposedly they announce us during the show."

"Wonderful." She wasn't looking to draw a lot of attention to herself, but didn't say anything as they were
ushered into the next room that she guessed was the show-

room when she saw the large arena. The room was set in a circle, with stadium seating separated into four sections by fancy metal gating that rose up to a cathedral ceiling. Each section had a designated color – red, black, blue, and white – that matched the color of the wooden tables and high-backed chairs.

The tables surrounded and looked down upon a stage of sand, an oval-shaped arena that was currently empty. At one end of the arena was a stage set on a high platform; at the other, what looked to Izz like a hallway was blocked off by a thick velvet curtain.

The lights were dim, with fog misting the ceiling and curling around the walls. A man dressed as a squire led them to their seats with a flashlight. As Olivia promised, they were front and center in the red section. Already an appetizer had been set on the table for the six of them to enjoy while everyone else was seated. Izz was all but manhandled into the middle seat, Olivia and Deanna on her immediate sides. She ignored their chatting while they waited for the show to begin, instead sipping her drink and wondering how hard it would be to duck out and hide in the bathroom, or maybe take a walk around the castle.

Before she could make an escape attempt, the lights dimmed further and a horn blasted from somewhere in the distance. A cheer rose up from the crowd – a full house, Izz realized, not having paid attention to anyone coming or going. Resigning herself to a long night, she fell back against the chair, resting her head on the soft cushion and watching as the show began with a horse race, then an introduction to the kingdom by two squires readying the arena while chatting with one another in some kind of skit. Izz couldn't help but roll her eyes at some of the historical inaccuracies and over-acting, but went with it for the sake of her friends.

Once the introduction was complete and the lights flashed, Izz shifted in her seat, feeling that something important was going to happen. An announcer that she couldn't see boasted of knights and victories, and then the first appeared.

"Now that is a damn sexy knight," Miley said on Izz's left, her eyes watching the blue knight as he rode a circle around the arena.

"He's the enemy, bozo!" Beth replied, smacking her friend on the shoulder. "We boo him, not let him know he's attractive."

Izz huffed, watching the knight make his pass. He certainly was attractive, albeit a little young for them, with thick blonde hair that was just the right amount of messy. His face was freshly shaved, his strong jaw and serious expression making him look the perfect level of deadly and boyish. The white knight came out behind him, white-blonde hair tied back with an elegant scarf, blue eyes bright, beard thick and neatly trimmed. Just after him was the black knight, a fitting color for his appearance – dark hair tightly curled together in waves more than halfway down his back, black beard at least three inches long, and the sun-kissed skin of a man who enjoyed being on the beach.

Izz watched them all through nearly unseeing eyes, taking in each one, clapping the appropriate amount, not really invested in the excitement of the crowd around her.

Then she saw the red knight. Their knight. Her knight.

He rode out on a horse blacker than midnight itself, a

strong, proud stallion with a thick mane that poofed perfectly in the breeze of each step. Her eyes traveled from horse to man, taking in the heavy black boots, crimson-red pants accented with black stitching, thick armor strapped across a strong chest and even stronger shoulders. A sword bounced with each horse step at his side, the metal glinting in the red-misted lights, reflecting across a face she swore was sculpted from stone. His expression was intense, dark eyes staring straight ahead at the other knights, thick shoulder-length black hair framing strong cheekbones and a dimpled chin, full lips set in a determined line, hard jaw set.

He was, without a doubt, the most intriguing and captivating man Izz had ever laid eyes upon.

The knight oozed confidence with every movement. Her gaze never left his face as he stopped right in front of them and faced their section, lifting his arms to the sound of whistles and cheers. Banners swung from the hands of fans as his black eyes scanned the crowd, eventually landing on her.

Izz sucked in a breath when the man offered the slightest of smiles and winked at her, then turned and took his place next to the other three knights. She blew out that breath, mentally chastising herself for staring, so caught up in the whirlwind of guilt and lust and intrigue warring within her that she didn't see the nudge Olivia gave Deanna, the sly grin Miley gave the twins.

Once all four knights were settled in place, a line of horse and man in the center of the arena, a curtain withdrew at the platform on the north end – the same direction the knights were facing. A man Izz recognized as the king entered to the sound of applause.

In turn, the king introduced the knights and their sto-ries. Izz didn't hear any of them, so focused as she was on their knight. His attention never left the king, and she took the opportunity to observe every inch of him, down to the way he gently stroked the horse, fingers trailing over the stallion's mane in a way that had Izz imagining what it would feel like if that were her hair, her neck being touched.

"And the last of our brave, daring knights of the kingdom, Knight Cadian of the North!" the king's voice rang through her musings.

Cadian, Izz mentally repeated to herself, shaking her-self out of her imagination and hoping her thoughts hadn't been obvious to anyone else. She liked the name, and wondered if it was the man's true name or merely a char-acter.

Forcing herself to focus, Izz watched as the king gave each of the knights a gift. The yellow knight, a rose the color of the morning sun. The black knight, a feather as dark as the mare he rode upon. The blue knight, a chain with a sapphire-colored pendant. And the red knight, a sash emblazoned with the mark of a dragon.

The knights broke away from the king then and moved toward their respective sections, bestowing one lucky maiden with the gift. Izz waited, expecting their knight to approach one of the little girls sitting around them, and was surprised when he stopped in front of their table. Miley let loose a loud catcall, prompting laughter from the surrounding tables, but the knight's stare was aimed only at Izz. He leaned forward slightly so he could reach across the railing and hand her the sash.

"For you, m'lady," he said, "a token of my appreciation for your gorgeous presence, and a promise that I shall win this battle for you."

Izz lifted a brow at the line that even he seemed to find amusing, but accepted the gift nonetheless. When he didn't move, but instead stared at her expectantly, she sighed and slipped the sash over her head and gave him a look that said he'd better be satisfied.

Apparently he was, because he rode off then and the battle began.

Despite herself, Izz was captivated by the show, fully engaged by the jousting and swordplay, horse racing and skills challenges. When the blue knight fought the villain, she looked forward to his victory. When the red knight, Knight Cadian, took a shield to the face, she gasped at the sight of blood and clapped when he got back up. And when he won in the end, she was secretly overjoyed.

"Looks like we got ourselves a champ!" Miley yelled over the roar of the red section, celebrating their win. She waved the Cadian banner high, despite the eye rolls she earned from her friends. Beth and Jackie joined in on the cheers, while Izz opted to stay seated but did offer a round of applause as she watched their knight parade around the arena in victory.

Confetti-type banners rained down from the ceiling through the misted fog, and the king approached Knight Cadian to gift him the princess's hand in marriage. That did earn another smirk from Izz, albeit a good-natured one. The show ended with the red knight riding off with his soon-to-be bride perched on the horse in front of him, and the crowd began filing out. Izz was the last to leave the table, picking at the remnants of dessert before trailing behind everyone else, casting a final glance down at the arena.

She followed her friends up the stairs, out of the showroom. The farther they walked, distancing themselves from the scent of horses and smoke and bloodshed, the more Izz actually missed the seat she'd occupied for the past two hours. Despite herself, she'd had a good time, forgetting her misery long enough to actually be interested in something other than her broken heart.

"Pictures!" Olivia demanded as they exited the arena and entered a new room filled with memorabilia. The space was brightly lit, with each corner of the room decked out in the color and crest of one of the performing knights.

"Pictures of what?" Izz asked as she glanced around, marveling once more at the décor and items from the world's past. She wondered how the owners of the place had secured such relics, though she guessed many of them were replicas. She preferred to pretend they were real, for her own amusement.

"Of our strapping knight, of course!" Olivia replied, pulling out her cell. "You didn't think we'd let you go without documenting your return to the living world, did you?"

As soon as the words left her mouth, Olivia regretted them. The expression on Izz's face changed from hesitant amusement to insult and sadness. "Girl, I'm sorry. I was just messing with you. One picture with handsome Knight Cadian. That's all we ask."

She could have been offended, punished her friend for such careless words, retreated back inside herself to that place of darkness. But, just this once, Izz would let her friend off the hook – and maybe make her pay for it later on. "Fine. One picture."

Relief spread across Olivia's face. She hooked her arm through Izz's and led the group to the large crowd that had gathered around the red knight. From their place in the back, they watched each picture and autograph, hearts melting over the little girls with princess crowns who timidly approached the knight and eyes rolling over the twenty-something women who pressed themselves against him and asked to touch his sword.

"I'm not doing that," Izz told her friends after the tenth or so woman asked for a kiss. So far, none of them had been granted their request, and their exaggerated disappointment entertained her. Instead, the knight named Cadian gave them a charming smile that made them wobbly at the knees and complimented them on their choice of wardrobe.

When it was her turn, Izz released a sigh and approached, ready to get the picture over with. She offered him a small nod.

"Good evening, m'lady," Knight Cadian greeted with that killer smile of his, the kind that made his eyes crinkle slightly at the corners of otherwise dark, hooded eyes. "As promised, I have won this battle for you."

Izz lifted a brow. "Maybe you should tell that to the princess you rode off with."

His grin only widened as he bowed. "And what is your name?"

"Isabella."

Isabella? she asked herself. She couldn't remember the last time she'd given someone her full name. "Uh … Izz."

His eyes widened slightly, as though understanding some deeper knowledge she wasn't privy to. "A beautiful

36

name, Isabella. I trust you enjoyed the battle?"

"I did," Izz answered honestly, his voice doing strange things to her thoughts. She'd never reacted so strongly to a man's voice before.

"It pleases me to hear this," he replied, taking her hand in his own and bringing it to his lips, kissing her knuckles lightly. Despite her firmly set jaw, Izz swallowed hard, warmth coursing through her at his touch.

Get it together, she ordered herself, pulling her hand back and turning so Olivia could take the picture. The knight wrapped an arm around her back, fitting her comfortably at his side. He was tall, but she had never been the shortest of the bunch, so her body molded to his in a way that nearly had her flushed.

After Olivia snapped the picture on her phone, Izz pulled away. "Well, nice to meet you," she said after a pause. She started to walk away, not ready to deal with the strange emotions welling up inside her, but was stopped in place by a gentle yet battle-roughened hand on her arm. Izz turned back to face him, about to tell off the stranger who dared to touch her, but something, perhaps that now annoyingly charming grin, made her pause.

"May I call on you?" he asked, his strong and confident tone from earlier that night fading into one that sounded almost … cautious, she realized.

After a pause, Izz released a deep breath and shook her head. "Thank you, but … that's … not a good idea."

Not offering him a second glance, Izz hurried away, nearly embarrassed by the weird hitch in her voice when she'd answered him. Her friends followed, not having heard what transpired but knowing *something* happened between the two.

"What was that about?" Olivia asked when they reached the first-floor landing. She glanced up the stairs at Knight Cadian, who was watching them descend. His attention was diverted by another group of people requesting pictures and autographs.

Izz shrugged. "Nothing. Just asked to 'call on me,' whatever that means."

"It means he likes what he saw," Beth put in with a grin. "And he's hot. You should go for it."

"I can't."

"Can't or won't?" Olivia challenged, crossing her arms when Izz gave her a steely glare. "Come on, Izz. A gorgeous specimen of the male species asks you out and you blow him off? No," she interrupted when Izz started to reply. "You have to at least go out to dinner with him. Or else."

Izz crossed her arms. "Or else what?"

Caught, Olivia shifted from foot to foot. Irritation spread through her when Izz started to leer. "Or else … Jackie and I won't plan any more of your events, and certainly not for a discount. You try finding people who can pull off your crazy-ass events as well as we can."

The two stared at one another, Izz ready to call her bluff, but seeing truth in Olivia's eyes. Smugness settled across her friend's face when Miley handed Izz a piece of paper. Izz broke her glare long enough to read her phone number and the hotel address already written on it. When she looked up, she saw five sets of eyes staring back at her, an unbreakable force. They had even formed a barrier between her and the door so she couldn't even flee like her head was screaming at her to do.

"You… I don't … But …I hate every single goddamn

one of you."

Both furious and nervous, Izz spun on her heel and marched back up the stairs. She didn't stop at the second-story landing, instead stalking across the floor and through the dwindling crowd still gathered around the red knight. He started to speak when he saw her, but the look on her face silenced him and so he simply waited to see what would happen.

Ignoring the protests around her, Izz pushed through the front row of people and didn't stop until she reached Knight Cadian. She paused for only a moment, long enough to slam a hand against his chest so that he was forced to mimic her action, taking the paper from her fingers.

"One date," she said, the words filled with more venom than she'd intended. She didn't wait to see his reaction, but if she did, she would have seen the way he watched her leave, the corners of his mouth flickering upward into a grin.

Chapter 6

SHE SPENT THE EVENING IGNORING her friends, locking herself in the master bedroom and focusing on her work. She could hear them on the other side of the door, laughing, goofing off, not at all concerned about the wrath of their hot-headed friend.

And why would they be, Izz scoffed to herself as she readied for bed. *They got what they wanted.*

By midnight she was tucked into bed, finally letting Olivia back in, lights off as she listened to the sound of the ocean. As much as she feared the sea, she loved the sound it made, the way it calmed her. To fall asleep to this melody was something she could get used to.

And fall asleep she did, into a troubled slumber where the ghost of her late husband came to her, asking of her intentions with this strange red knight, wondering why she was so willing to move on.

Not willing, she wanted to scream, but in her dream state she could only plead with her eyes for him to stay, just this once, just this moment. To be with her, to take away the loneliness and solitude that had become her life. But, just like he always did in her dreams, he left, disappearing into a cloud of white that left her completely alone.

Those feelings of hurt fled when she opened her eyes, the banging at the door overpowering any other thought and emotion. She tried to ignore it, but when the person kept on knocking she rose with an aggravated growl and threw on a robe to cover her ratty pajamas. Not bothering to smooth down her hair or check to make sure her 'fresh out of bed' look was appropriate for the general public, Izz wrenched open the bedroom door and marched through the living room. All was silent, her friends still sleeping off their hangover. Not even the knocking would stir them at this horribly early hour.

"What the hell do you–"

Izz stopped short when she saw who was on the other side of the door. Red Knight Cadian stood before her, dressed in a pair of jeans complemented by heavy boots and a dark-blue, short-sleeved button-down shirt, his black hair tied back at the nape of his neck. A brown leather band was wrapped around his left wrist, while the edges of a tattoo snaked out from his shirtsleeves. Izz hated that she wanted to see the whole thing, and that she had the urge to show off her own.

"Isabella," he said when she made no move to invite him in. "Is this a bad time?"

His deep voice had lost the accent from the previous night, but none of the smoothness. "It's like seven in the morning. What the hell do you think?" He only grinned, bringing forth a huff of exasperation out of her. "What are you doing here?"

"You owe me a date."

She stared at him for a moment, confused and trying

41

to clear the sleepy fog from her mind. "I thought you meant, like, dinner."

His grin widened. "You never set the terms for the date, m'lady." He knew he had her by the frown she sent his way. "I'll wait for you to get dressed. Wear comfy shoes."

"Why?"

He didn't answer, so, to annoy him as much as he was annoying her, she closed the door in his face and purposely took her time getting ready. Olivia was up by the time she was dressed, following her to the door, giddy with excitement. Izz considered telling her to go on the damn date herself if she was that excited about it.

"Keep her out as long as you can," Olivia said with a wink to the man still waiting on the front mat, shoving Izz out the door and locking it behind her.

"Traitor," Izz muttered beneath her breath, then looked up at her date for the morning. "So, before this goes any further, what's your name?"

"Cade."

"Oh … So all you knights go by your real names?"

Cade shrugged. "Some of us do. My *real* name is Roarke Cadian, but I've been known as Cade since I was a child."

His speech switched from formal to common and back to formal, she noticed. "Well, I've been known as Izz since I was a child, so none that that *Isabella* shit."

"Isabella is a beautiful name. But," he added when she frowned again, "Izz it is."

"Good." She ignored the arm he offered and started walking down the hall toward the elevators, wondering if the silence was as uncomfortable to him as it was to her.

Once they reached his car, she asked, "So, where are we going?"

"You let me worry about that, m'lady," Cade said with another of his trademark winks. "You wait right there; I'll get the door."

Ignoring him, Izz opened the door herself and hopped in while he merely shook his head. She started to ask him again where they were going, then decided to just roll with it. Once, in another life, she never would have asked for a plan. She would have simply hopped in the passenger seat, rolled down the window, and let the road take her where it may. She missed that life, the woman she once was who was so open to fun. So, today, she would try to find the person she used to be.

He took her out for breakfast at a quaint little bakery not far from the hotel. There weren't many people at the booths, so they chose one toward the back, beside a window that looked out at the sea. He ordered a coffee and meal of pancakes and eggs, she a Coke and breakfast of French toast.

"Soda girl, huh?"

"Coke all the way," Izz answered. "Love the smell of coffee, hate the taste." She'd never been good at small talk, and wondered what to say next. "So, um, tell me about yourself?"

Cade sat back, amused by her social awkwardness. He could tell how uncomfortable she was, how unsure she felt about his very presence. But, he also sensed interest – the same interest he felt about her. Sure, he'd played up his character during the show, but as soon as he kissed her hand, he felt it, that something special he'd been waiting for all his life. This woman, in all her standoffish and awkward glory, was *her*.

"I'm pretty average," he answered her question while pouring syrup over a pancake. "Thirty-three, never married, no kids, grew up in the rural northeast and moved down here as soon as I turned eighteen. I went to school in the area, found my place as a knight fighting for the damsel in distress." He shot her a quick grin. "My family has an interesting history going way, way back. Suffice it to say, my childhood was rooted in legends and mythology, so working at *Quest* is second nature to me."

She wanted to ask about this childhood of legends and mythology, partly out of interest and partly so he would keep talking. Embarrassment flooded her at the fact that she sounded like a silly schoolgirl with a first crush, but, damn it, the guy was smooth. Maybe too smooth.

"Not too bad a gig," she replied before she realized what she was saying. "Handsome knight battling evil villains, charming all the ladies while they get their picture taken. You must have built up quite the fanbase."

He knew what she was asking, but rather than be insulted, decided to make her work for the answer for his own amusement. "So you think I'm handsome?"

"What? No, I … I mean… Well, fuck." Izz blew out a breath, not sure if she should be embarrassed or irritated, or something else entirely. "I just meant–"

"That all the handsome knights take home a damsel after every show."

"I didn't say that."

"You didn't have to." He had her there. She *did* presume it, even if she didn't say it. "For what it's worth, I don't."

"I'm sure you get a lot of offers." Izz chastised herself as soon as she said it, though supposed it was a compliment of sorts.

Cade laughed, the sound both soothing and enticing to her ears. "We get our fair share, yes. It's entertaining, really. Some of our guests are weird in a good way, those just looking to goof around and pretend to be a maiden for a couple hours. Others are weird in a scary way, the ones who drink far too much and slip their numbers or room keys into our pockets during a picture." At the disgusted look on her face, he laughed again. "Most of the guys have girlfriends. It's all part of the job. Me, I prefer a woman who makes me work for it."

Izz wasn't sure how to answer, never having been much good at flirting. So, she merely dropped her gaze to her food. Cade watched her for a moment before continuing. "So, your turn. Tell me about yourself, aside from your charming conversational skills."

Izz made a face at him, but nearly laughed. For all her recklessness and outgoing ways of the past, she really did suck at basic conversations. It was a miracle she'd ever made it past any first date at all. "Um, well. My name is Isabella Nevear, but everyone calls me Izz." She saw how he perked up ever so slightly at her name, but chose to ignore it – for now. "Twenty-eight, live in California, was dragged to Myrtle Beach by a group of insane women hell bent on getting me out of the house for a few days. I don't know much about my family's history, though my father loved to tell stories."

"Loved?"

Izz bit back a sigh. "Yeah. He and my mom died when I was thirteen in a car accident. Freak accident, wet roads, crappy tires. It's fine." She waved a hand at him

45

when he started to offer his condolences.

"Thirteen is so young," Cade said instead. "What did you do after?"

"Lived with my grandma. Pretty much the most awful woman you'll ever meet. The kind who wouldn't cook you dinner unless you cleaned the entire house and slapped you across the face for saying 'yeah' instead of 'yes.'" Izz didn't have many good memories of those years, and for the life of her couldn't figure out why she was telling Cade, a complete stranger, all of this. Yet, her mouth wouldn't stop. "The day I turned eighteen I lit out of there faster than she could blink. Olivia and I had saved up for years and had enough to get our own place. It was rough for a while, but we made it."

"So you did." Cade offered her a smile. "I know you don't want condolences, but I am sorry for what you went through. I grew up with a big family and it was hard moving so far away from them. My sister ended up joining me after a while, which was nice. To not have that." He shook his head, feeling the conversation getting away from him and turning dark. "Sorry, I just meant that it couldn't have been easy, and you must be one tough chick."

Izz shrugged. "That's life."

There was so much more he wanted to say to comfort her, but she didn't seem the type to seek soothing words from men she barely knew. "So … kids? Have them, want them?"

Well that's mighty personal, she thought, trying hard not to roll her eyes. "No kids. Wouldn't mind them, but I can't have any." At his curious expression, she continued, careful to leave out any mention of her late husband. That, was far too personal. "Doctors aren't sure why. They just say my body won't allow it. It used to upset me, but I've accepted it. If I want to be a mother, I'll get a puppy, I guess."

Way to make it awkward, Izz, she chided herself. "Anyway, that's pretty much it."

Cade eyed her with a small grin. "Oh, I doubt that."

They chatted for a while longer about mostly impersonal things. The waitress appeared once their plates were mostly empty, placing the check facedown on the table before clearing away their plates. Cade moved the check away when Izz went to reach for it. "Don't think so, m'lady. Today is my treat. No protesting allowed."

Izz sat silently while he paid, enjoying the way his brows knit together as he calculated the tip, the way he loosened the band around his hair so that the thick locks framed his face. Once they rose from the table, Izz followed him back to the car, where he announced they were going on a tour of the beach town.

"You know, you really don't need to feel like you have to do this," Izz said when she got in the car. Cade paused in the act of starting it, sending her a confused frown. "Look, I'm not stupid. I saw Liv talking to some official-looking guy before the show, and then you just happen to single me out for the sash thing, *and* ask me out? Come on. There is no way you are putting up with someone like me for the fun of it. You're doing this as a favor to them. I'm just not entirely sure why."

For a moment, the car was silent. Then Cade sighed, and Izz knew she was right. "You can take me home now, if you want."

Shaking his head, Cade faced her again. "You're right, they did ask. They asked that whatever knight was

47

assigned to their group give you a little extra attention. Make you smile, I believe was their exact request. So, yes, that's what I did."

"I figured you planned this whole day because of them."

"Then you figured wrong." Cade lifted a shoulder in a boyish shrug. "They asked that I make the show exciting for you, not that I ask you out."

"Then ... why did you?"

Cade reached over and brushed a few tendrils of blonde hair away from her face. For once, Izz wasn't overcome with the need to slap that hand away. "Because as soon as I saw you, I wanted to do more than make you smile. I wanted to know who you were."

Smooth, too smooth, she told herself again, and hated that she was moved by his words. But she'd already insulted him once on their short date, and didn't want to do so again. "Okay then, Knight Cade. Make me smile."

Chapter

7

HE MADE TRUE ON HIS promise to show her the town, highlighting the tourist hotspots as well as the lesser-known beaches. Around lunchtime he stopped at one of those beaches, though only after promising they would return later to the zipline course they passed earlier that day. Izz may have been grouchy and aloof at times, but she was a sucker for anything that gave her a rush.

"Alright, m'lady, the beach awaits."

She helped Cade carry out a basket and bundle of towels from the parking lot to the beach. It was fairly quiet at this location, and she wondered if it was a private park of sorts. Once they picked out a spot, Cade laid down a blanket and invited her to sit.

"I only brought snacks," he told her, gesturing to the basket. "Figured I'd keep you hungry for dinner."

"Dinner?" she repeated, setting her phone down on the blanket next to her and casually checking the time. "Mighty long date you've planned."

Cade opened the basket and pulled out a few paper plates. "Can't end the date yet, still working on getting that smile."

She shot him a smirk instead and accepted the plate he offered, filling it with an assortment of fruit and cheeses. "Nice spread."

"And to top it off," he replied, pulling out two plastic bottles, "you have your choice between apple juice or white wine. I didn't know if you are a drinker."

Izz considered her options, then took the apple juice. "Sometimes I drink, but only with people I know I can trust." She realized the insult in her words instantly. "I mean–"

"No offense taken," Cade laughed. "Give me a few hours yet."

It would take more than a few hours for her to let her guard down, but Izz let him think whatever he wanted. They ate the spread before them, chatting casually about last night's show and some of the other knights. She liked listening to him, was caught up in the way his mouth moved, how animated his hands were. She'd noticed those hands last night during his battles, dreamed about them even. Today, she was still wondering what it was about this man that had invaded her senses, that made everything seem okay, like her misery was just a forgotten feeling of the past. That pull frightened and excited her all at once.

"How long have you been in town?" Cade asked suddenly, changing the topic so quickly that it took Izz a few seconds to readjust.

"Um ... since Wednesday."

"Taken a dip yet? The great blue," he explained when she just stared at him.

Izz cast a glance over at the ocean, at the waves lapping gently against the shore. "Oh, no. I don't go in the water."

"Why not?"

"Sea monsters."

Cade stared at her for a moment, trying to determine if she was being serious or not. When her expression didn't falter even the slightest, he frowned. "Sea monsters," he repeated slowly, eyes taking on a faraway look that she didn't understand but was curious about all the same. "Like what?"

Izz turned her attention to the water. The waves were calm, not at all threatening on the surface. "Like, killer squid and sharks and … stuff that wants to eat you. I'm serious!" she said a little louder when he grinned over at her. "I used to have nightmares as a kid. Up through my teenage years, actually. Awful dreams about being on this old ship, surrounded by sea monsters taking apart the boat piece by piece. Sometimes I was alone, other times with people I'd never seen before but knew as family in the dream. Regardless, the result was always the same. We all died." Izz blew out a breath, not enjoying the trip back into her childhood nightmares. "In any case, I stay out of the water."

Wondering how he'd react to her confession, she dared a look at Cade, only to find him deep in thought. She waved a hand in front of his face. "Where'd you go?" she asked. "I thought *I* spaced out a lot."

Cade shook his head and sat up straighter. "Nowhere. Just thinking."

"About what? Hey, I'm nosy," Izz said when he lifted a brow at her question.

"About how it's time to introduce you to the great blue."

Izz scoffed. "Don't count on it, Knight Cadian."

"Ah, but what kind of knight in shining armor would I be if I didn't help my damsel overcome her fears?" Cade leapt to his feet in one fluid motion, pulling Izz up before she realized what was happening. Not giving her time to protest, he tucked her in his arms, one under her knees and the other around her back.

"Cade! Don't even – put me down!" Her voice was laced with both panic and anger, but he ignored her protests. "What the fuck are you–"

Her words were drowned out by the water that splashed up against her face. Izz's arms went around Cade's neck in fear, his laughter echoing in her ears as her fingers tightened on his shirt. The water crept higher, from his legs to her back to her shoulders.

"You son of a bitch," she muttered in a shaky tone, hating that she was trembling, that she was clinging to him like the damsel she'd allowed herself to become. Her eyes closed against the sea, head turned so that her face was buried in his shoulder.

Cade's arms tightened around her as guilt crept into his chest. He'd misjudged her fear, thinking she was overplaying her nightmares that he'd assumed no longer haunted her. Now he was paying the price for his misinterpretation, and had to make amends even as he mentally chastised himself for being such an ass. He loved the feel of her arms around him, but not the reason why they were there.

"It's okay," he whispered, lowering his head so that his cheek was pressed against her temple. "You're safe with me. You always were, you always will be."

She heard the words, but couldn't process them. Not with images of fangs and blood swimming through her thoughts. But she did feel the warmth of his body against her own, despite the cold water soaking through her clothes, and she let that warmth comfort her.

They stood there, chest high in the water, for only a moment longer. Her arms still around Cade's neck, Izz opened her eyes and looked around. The water was smooth, the waves not breaking this far out, no people around to disturb the silence. The sun was warm on her face, the ocean cold beneath the surface.

"I want to go back," she demanded and Cade obliged, keeping her in his arms until they were on the shore. Once her feet touched sand, Izz immediately took a few steps away and looked up at him. "I'm not sure if I should thank you, or punch you."

"You're welcome to do both." He stood perfectly still, hands in his pockets, while she eyed him, contemplating, and hated that she'd moved away from him. Although, he had to admit he couldn't blame her. "For what it's worth, I take full responsibility for being a complete ass."

"Uh-huh." Izz took another step back, wringing water out of her shirt. "Tell you what, you find me some dry clothes and I'll spare you a black eye."

Cade reached for her hand, though she didn't let him take it. "Now that, I can take care of."

SHE EXPECTED CADE TO LEAD her back to the car, and was surprised when he packed up their picnic and started down the beach. Tired of asking questions, and a little embarrassed by her display of cowardice in the water, Izz fell into step beside him, trusting that he was leading her somewhere that *wouldn't* end in her untimely demise.

Even as she thought the words, she laughed at them in her head. For some strange reason, she almost trusted this too-smooth man with his tall, dark, and handsome aura. The way he stared at her, the way her body responded to his touch, was hard to ignore. She'd always been a good judge of character, and right now, she was sure his character was one of worth.

Doubt crept into her thoughts when he started to lead her up the dunes to a two-story house set back on the shore. "Whose place is this?"

"Beats me." Cade laughed when Izz drew back. "Kidding. It's my place."

Izz craned her neck and took in the house. It was an intriguing mix of modern and exotic, with large bay windows overlooking the back and an actual tower along the north side. She really wanted to know what was in the tower, if anything at all. The walls showed a beautiful stone façade that matched the ash-gray shingles, which ended at eaves that curled up at the corners of the roof.

"Not bad, Knight Cadian. Show business has been kind to you."

Cade shrugged as they ascended the back deck steps. "It helps that I co-own the entire place."

She wanted to ask for details, but he was already inside, and she followed with only the slightest of hesitations. The inside was every bit as impressive as the exterior, with an interesting mix of modern décor and medieval flair. Hardwood lined the floors as far as she could see, adorned with intricate rugs of all colors that matched the textured walls and iron sconces holding makeshift torches topped with orange lights.

They stopped just inside the back door and Cade

kicked off his shoes, removing his shirt at the same time to avoid dripping on the floor. Izz tried not to stare at the display of muscle before her, and was slightly disappointed that his back was angled away from her so she couldn't see his tattoo. "Wait here," he ordered. "I'll get you some clothes."

He disappeared up the stairs. It only took a few seconds for her to grow bored and wander farther into the house. As she walked down the hall, a flash of silver caught her eye. Izz stopped and peered into what she guessed was a living room or den. The far wall was lined with swords and daggers, small and large, thick and thin, elegantly handled and crudely designed. It was a collection that called to her, impressed as much as it frightened her, and all at once she was filled with the urge to hold every single one of them. So much so that she shoved her hands in her wet pockets to prevent herself from ruining what looked like a magnificent display.

Her blue eyes scanned over every sword until they reached a blank space in the wall, as though that single space was waiting for the last piece of the puzzle. Absurdly, she thought of her own sword and wondered how it would look hanging next to all of these incredible relics of history.

"I didn't have you pegged as a history buff," a deep voice said behind her.

Izz spun around, caught with her hand mid-air as she nearly did what she always yelled at her friends for doing – touching the swords. "I'm not," she answered. "I just have a thing for swords." She nearly told him about her own, but something held her back, as though that one relic from her own past was something special to be kept between the people she loved and trusted most.

Cade eyed her curiously, assessing her answer. "Perhaps one day we can have ourselves a battle. Not with these," he said quickly when Izz glanced over at the wall. "I have a selection of practice swords that will do nicely for sparring."

"Uh-huh." She was slightly weirded out by the conversation, and yet excited at the same time. She wanted to practice, to hold the metal between her hands, clash sword against sword, dance around him while sweat and blood dripped from their bodies.

Izz cleared her throat and stepped away from the wall, somewhat disappointed that he'd put on a fresh, dry shirt. "So, you got any clothes or what?"

Cade tossed her a pair of pants and shirt, along with a bathing suit. "My sister keeps some things here for when she visits. Change into those while I dry your wet clothes." He lifted a brow when Izz merely stared down at the clothing. "Not your style? I'd be happy to give you a pair of boxers."

His frown turned into a grin when she turned on her heel and stalked from the room.

CADE WATCHED THE WOMAN WALK away, leaving her to her own devices to find the bathroom. She intrigued him, the way she was so easy to rile up, so calm one minute and bitchy the next, the way she was clearly holding something back yet tried so hard to appear strong.

Her friends had asked that he make her feel special, to make her smile. But they hadn't said *why* she needed to smile. Something had happened to her, and, from the moment he saw her, he wanted to know what. He wanted to make it better.

And that worried him. Not because he didn't want her, but because he'd never felt such a close connection with anyone before, let alone a woman he'd just met. Cade didn't believe in love at first sight, and still didn't, but every part of him was telling him not to let Izz walk away so easily. Some part of his soul seemed to recognize this particular woman, and even though his head told him he needed to be careful, to tread lightly with someone who was essentially a stranger, his heart shouted at him to never let her go. To save her, from whatever she needed saving.

"No offense to your sister, but this is the ugliest shirt I've ever seen."

Izz's irritated voice tone cut into his thoughts. He turned to the doorway to see her pulling at the collar of the pink silk top, which ruffled at the bottom and was accented by embroidered white flowers. The color contrasted her skin and made her look like a teenager playing dress-up. It was so unsuiting of her that he had to laugh. The sound only annoyed her further.

"You're welcome to take it off," he told her with a wink. She only smirked at him and tossed her wet clothes at his chest.

"Dry these so I can get out of the world's worst excuse for a shirt."

He did as she asked, tossing her clothes in the dryer before leading her out to the back deck, which overlooked the ocean. When she leaned back against the railing, staring at him curiously, he tried to force out the memory of having her undergarments in his hands only moments ago.

"What?" he finally asked when she continued to stare.

Izz narrowed her eyes thoughtfully, slightly annoyed with herself for being taken in by his brooding yet laughing gaze. There was something familiar about those eyes, as though she'd spent a lifetime staring into them.

Stop being weird, she chastised herself, and forced her brain to make something up. "Nothing. I was just wondering … If you co-own the business and clearly do well at it, why are you *in* the show?"

"Because it's fun." His answer was instant and honest. Her eyes never left his face as he continued. "I enjoy it. Good exercise, get to fight with swords, great co-workers. There's great camaraderie among us, so even if we beat the shit out of each other for the show, we laugh about it and razz each other later. Most of them are younger than me, but it's no secret I'm the best." He grinned at her as he puffed out his chest a bit. The corner of one side of her mouth quirked, but barely. "They're good guys. Most are in college so they don't stick around. They all have big dreams, and *Quest* helps them achieve them. I stick around because I love it."

And because it's the core of who I am, he added silently, not ready to reveal that part of himself just yet.

"Huh." She turned her gaze to the ocean, staring at the swells building in the distance. Despite her earlier venture in the water, it still scared the hell out of her. "So—"

Her words were cut off in a rush when Cade took hold of her arm and tugged her against him, pressing her against his solid chest and wrapping an arm around her back before lowering his face to hers.

She wanted to protest, but just as the curse formed on her tongue, his own met hers. All thought and sense left her in a flood of abandonment, replaced by an explosion of color behind her closed eyes. In those colors she saw flashes of a life that could be: midnight swims in an eastern ocean, bonfires surrounded by people she didn't yet know but wanted to nonetheless, a man with black eyes staring down at her with admiration. Her hands lifted to his chest as she melted into the sensation of those images, feeling the warm embrace of a comfort she didn't realize until just now she'd been longing for all her life.

That thought jarred Izz out of the moment and she pulled back, yanking herself from Cade's hold with a slight gasp. Her hand went to her mouth, fingers pressed against swollen lips, guilt and want warring within her as he stared down at her with those same emotions reflected in his eyes.

"Isabella—" he started, but she cut him off.

"I'm sorry, I have to go," she insisted, wrenching herself free and all but leaping off the deck after grabbing her phone from the railing, rushing across the sand to her escape.

AFTER A LONG WALK BACK to the hotel, Izz stomped into the room, furious with herself for letting a man who was basically a stranger get that close to her, even angrier that she let herself enjoy his kiss. And the visions she saw behind her eyes … that couldn't be normal.

It had been a long time since a man had touched her in any way. Over a year since she'd felt lips upon her own. Surely, she justified to herself, that was the explanation for … whatever it was she was feeling. Her body told her it was lust, a deep need for the man who posed as a knight in shining armor, but her mind rationalized she was just lonely. She didn't believe that love just happened. You had to work for it, deserve it. Let attraction mold into something greater until she was completely consumed by the dark-haired knight who gifted her a silly sash all to make her smile.

Izz scoffed at her own foolish thoughts and headed for her room, thankful the girls were out. She passed by the mirror and stopped short. "Shit," she cursed when she saw her reflection, the hideous pink shirt. Now she'd have to see Cade again. She could almost live with losing her own clothes, but there was some annoying need ingrained within her to do the right thing and return something that didn't belong to her.

For now, she stripped off the borrowed apparel and took a quick shower, washing off the memories of the day before toweling off and changing into her own clothes. Her body craved a nap, but just as she sat on the bed she heard the door open and the sound of five over-excited women met her ears.

"Izz!" Olivia saw her first through the open door, and her expression immediately soured into one of annoyance. "Why are you back so soon? Did you seriously run him off?"

"Not now, Olivia," Izz replied with a sigh. Olivia must have heard the pain in the sound because the look in her eyes changed to one of concern.

"What happened?"

"Nothing."

Olivia entered the room and shut the door behind her, closing out the other three. She sat on the bed next to Izz. "Seriously, what happened? Was he a dick? I'll kick his ass if he was."

Izz nearly smiled, having seen her friend do just that in the past. "No, he was pretty much the perfect gentleman."

"So … what's the issue?" Olivia prodded when her friend fell silent.

Izz wrestled with telling her, worried about exposing her own vulnerabilities. But, the truth was, she was tired of keeping it all inside, of no longer having anyone there to listen, to be her shoulder. "He kissed me."

Olivia waited, but Izz didn't offer any further explanation. She wasn't sure what her friend was looking for as a response. "How was it?"

"The best kiss of my life," Izz confessed. "And that's the problem." At her friend's stare, Izz held up her hands and dropped them in frustration. "Olivia, I haven't been with anyone since Eric died. In this life and the next, that's what we said to each other on our wedding day. I feel like I betrayed him."

Olivia slid an arm around Izz's shoulders even though she knew her friend hated close contact. "Izz, that's the kind of thing you say to the person you love. And you do mean it, when you're with them. You never think of what comes next if something happens to one of you. But you know as well as I do that he wouldn't want you to be alone the rest of your life. You can't betray someone who isn't actually in this life anymore."

"Then I'm betraying his memory."

"You know that's not true," Olivia argued, having had this same fight with her friend several times in the past. "Look. Feel what you need to feel. It's not right and it's not wrong. It's just feelings and you have to work through them. But don't let it stop you from living your life, you know?"

The two sat in silence for a moment, one contemplating her friend's words and the other hoping she never had to experience the heartache of the one sitting next to her. Finally, after she couldn't take it anymore, Izz leapt to her feet.

"Let's go out tonight."

She didn't need to say another word. Olivia was already making arrangements.

THEY ATE AT A FANCIER restaurant in town, Olivia
and Beth filling up on drinks and Izz pushing around her
steak, her stomach still in knots from the day's events. As
they exited, the twins pushing one another and complain-
ing about the humidity, Izz shoved her hands in her thin
jacket's pockets and fell in step behind the group. They
walked along the main street searching for something to
do, some kind of trouble to get into. It was vacation, after
all.

As they strolled, Izz glanced around, taking in the
sights of the city at night. Tourists milled around, some
hand in hand with their significant other, others holding
children on their shoulders, and more still out in groups
just like her. Buildings were lit up with neon signs, arcades
and ice cream shops and what looked like blacklight mini-
golf. She made a mental note to check that one out. She
was a sucker for mini-golf.

"Here we go," Olivia announced as she came to a
stop outside a small hut of a building. The wall to the right
was painted red and black in an ominous portrait of what
looked like Hell. A long, narrow, dimly lit staircase sat

next to the wall, and at the top Izz could hear screaming.

Well, that's a good sign, she thought wryly, and soon discovered the source of the screams when a group of teenage girls burst into view at the top of the stairs, their shouts turning into giggles.

On the other side of the stairs and Hell wall, a man stood behind a desk made of bamboo and fiberglass bones, which, surprisingly, looked amazingly real. The man was tall and thick, with twisted black dreads that fell halfway down his back and matched the black of his tattered robes. When his stare met hers, Izz saw, with some amount of unease, that his eyes were completely white, a stark contrast to his dark skin.

"You have come to Death's Door," he boomed out in a voice that rattled her bones, startling Jackie, always the scaredycat. "Do you ladies wish to take your chances amongst the house of horrors?"

"Hell yes!" Olivia and Miley cried just as the twins muttered out, "Uh, no thanks."

Those milky-white eyes turned to Izz, ignoring Deanna altogether. "It seems you are the deciding vote, though I'd hate to see such a pretty face get lost in the horrors just past Death's Door."

"Perhaps she just needs a knight to guide her," a deep voice said from behind.

Izz stilled, knowing that voice, unable to forget it. Just before she turned, she steeled her gaze on Olivia, who gave her a shrug that defied the grin she was trying to suppress. *Ever the matchmaker*, Izz thought, giving her friend a look that said she'd deal with her later – and throw her phone in the ocean.

He stood on the sidewalk looking like the dashing

knight she already knew he was, in a pair of dark wash jeans and a short-sleeved, navy-blue shirt that showed off the body he worked hard to build. His feet were clad in what almost looked like cowboy boots, which amused her, and his hair was loose, framing his face in shadows that were irritatingly alluring.

The sparks flashed again at the memory of his lips on hers just hours ago, but she dowsed them with a sigh. "I don't need a protector." It was the first thing that came to mind when she finally shook her gaze from the sight of him. She heard snickering at his side and realized he wasn't alone. Two other men stood with him and, after a moment, she recognized them as knights from the show.

"*Quest* field trip?" she asked, hoping her question sounded as snotty as she meant it. The guy may make her knees weak, but that didn't mean she had to accept it.

"Something like that," he replied easily, mouth lifting into that now-familiar smirk. "Good thing too, as it seems we are needed to guide those foolish enough to dare Death's Door."

Smooth, too smooth, Izz scoffed to herself while the girls looked on in a mix of unease and entertainment. "Your guidance is not needed, good sir. I think I'll brave the horrors alone."

"I insist, m'lady." Cade handed the man in dreads a wad of cash, enough to cover entrance for them all. The man gestured for them to pass through a door, and Izz strode through first simply to be a pain in the ass. She heard him chuckling as he followed.

When all nine of them were inside the small, dark room lined with weird gray walls, a light flashed in front of them and another man appeared in a booth. His face was lit up with white streaks that glowed in the dark.

"Welcome, welcome, my sweet victims," he greeted, his tone a raspy southern drawl. "Hell awaits those who seek adventure in the shadows." At that he laughed, the lights flickering in tune with his chuckling. Izz saw Beth and Jackie jump and cling to one another at her side. On her other side, Deanna took in a deep breath and moved a step closer.

"Follow the rules and you might just live. Be a hero and succumb to the fires of Hell." The host banged on the desk, making them all jump. "And just remember, the walls tell secrets ... so you might just find a way to cheat your way out of Hell."

At that he let loose a cackling roar and gestured with a grand sweep of his arm. Fog rose up in the corner of the room and a back gaping hole in the wall appeared, beckoning them forward. "Enter, if you dare!"

Her stomach lurched ever so slightly when she stepped through the doorway, pushing back black strips of cloth that clung to her skin. Strobe lights combined with stripe-painted walls disoriented her, but she pushed through, putting on a brave front and keeping Cade to her back.

The others fell back as she continued forward, but their screams bounced off the walls, echoing from room to room. Around corners she spun, heart pounding against her chest with each moan and garbled shout and clawed hand that reached out from the walls.

Izz gasped when some sort of mutated black blob shot out in front of her, crawling across the floor after sending a screeching scowl in her direction. Lights flashed red, fog surrounding her, Olivia's scream from somewhere behind merging with Miley's. At her side, Cade tugged on her arm to keep her moving. He started to lead her toward a shadowed doorway, but she turned, concerned for her friends.

"Wait, I want to see where–"

Her words turned into a shriek when a man burst through a doorway they had just passed with a shout. Izz tumbled backward into Cade, who gripped her arms to steady her.

"Are you okay?" he asked, concern turning to humor when he saw that she was no longer screaming, but, instead, was laughing. Even in the shadows of the haunted house, her face lit up with the shine of happiness, of letting go, of being in the moment. She laughed at herself, at her absurdity, and he was completely enraptured with the sight of such a smile. Some part of him wished he could be the cause of that light, rather than it being the result of a man trying to scare the hell out of her.

All too soon, she shook off her amusement and continued on. Behind her, she heard her friends screaming for help, which nearly made her laugh again as she decided to let them figure it out on their own. "Come on, we have to beat them out."

Not even realizing what she was doing, Izz grabbed hold of Cade's arm and pulled him forward, deeper into the winding walls. Something dark and spindly dropped from the ceiling, making them both yell in surprise and run away, hands flailing as they searched for the way out. Soon they came to a dead end, the only way to go to either left or right.

She saw something on the wall, a flash of color just above her eye's level. Squinting, Izz saw an arrow painted on the wall, so faint that she wondered how she could make it out at all. The arrow pointed in the opposite direction that Cade was going.

"This way," she argued, pointing to the door to the left.

"No, this way." He gestured to the dark hallway on the right.

She glanced down that hall, peering through the darkness to see what looked like another dead end. Izz was surprised he couldn't see it, but hell if she would tell him that. "Fine then, a wager. You go your way, I'll go mine."

"Winner gets what?"

"Name your terms upon your victory."

He considered for only a second before shaking her hand. "You're on."

Two minutes later, he emerged through the exit door to find Izz leaning against the opposite wall, arms crossed and one brow lifted in an expression of smugness.

"How did you know?" he asked as he approached, slightly breathless. She only shrugged. "How?"

"The walls tell secrets," she repeated the host's earlier words. "The way out was written on the walls."

"It was so dark in there. How did you see that?" She only shrugged again. For a moment Cade wondered if his mother was right and he really did need glasses, but didn't have time for further speculation since Izz was currently gloating in front of him. "Alright then, what are your terms?"

Before she could answer, Beth and Jackie burst through the door, holding one another and laughing hysterically in an identical fit of terror mixed with fun. Deanna trailed behind them with one of the knights on her arm, then Olivia and Deanna. "Where's the other one?" Izz asked, realizing she didn't know Cade's friends' names.

Olivia gestured back inside Death's Door. "He got lost. Hell won."

It took a few minutes but the third man finally appeared, looking a bit sheepish and worse for wear. "Got turned around," he muttered to the sound of the girls' razzing.

Satisfied that they were all safe and accounted for, Cade turned back to Izz. "Your terms, m'lady."

One corner of her mouth turned up in a smirk. "I'll let you know," she answered, then left the men behind, leading her friends down the long, narrow stairwell and back into the mix of the city at night.

SHE STOOD ON THE SHORELINE, toes just out of reach of the salty waters, arms crossed as she stared out at the horizon. Dawn brought with it gorgeous pinks and purples and oranges that lit up the morning sky, reflecting off the smooth ocean like a stained-glass window.

As she watched the sun rise, Izz thought over the past few days. She'd been dragged across the country to Myrtle Beach, forced into a date with a man her friends thought was cute, kissed by that same man, and led through a crappy haunted house that resulted in her winning whatever she wanted.

And, damn it, what she wanted made her feel guilty as hell.

"Why are you up so ungodly early?" a voice whined behind her. Izz didn't need to turn to know Olivia was trudging down the beach, most likely with a large mug of coffee in hand. "No one in their right mind is awake right now."

"The sun's awake," Izz answered absently.

Olivia took a sip of coffee – from a decidedly large mug, Izz noticed from the corner of her eye – and sighed. "You're thinking again, aren't you?"

"So?"

"So, stop it. Whatever you are debating, just do it." Olivia lifted a brow when Izz turned a frown in her direction. "Seriously. You used to always just go with your gut. You got soft."

"So you keep saying."

"Tell me I'm wrong."

Izz wanted to argue, but deep down she knew her friend was right. Marriage *had* made her soft, always trying to fit the mold of a perfect wife, be the kind of woman her husband could be proud of.

But she didn't have a husband anymore. She wasn't a wife. She was just a lonely woman standing on the beach waging a war between her head and her heart.

With a wry grin, Izz turned back to Olivia. "Got plans for tonight?"

Chapter 10

CADE STRAPPED A WIDE LEATHER belt around his waist, leaning over to lace up his boots. He was a bit early for the show, but wanted to get in a little practice before the doors opened. For fun, more so than necessity.

He'd been telling the truth when he told Izz that he worked for fun. At thirty-three, he'd been co-owner of *Quest for Avalon* for ten years now, partnering with his father, who started the business with a dream of showcasing history throughout the years. *Quest* was primarily a show about knights, but depending on the day and season was known to cycle in shows with gladiators and wizards, just for the entertainment of mixing it up. Cade wasn't typically in those shows, as he preferred swordplay over wands. His family history went back to the Middle Ages on both his parents' sides, and they took it seriously.

It was a history he wasn't quite ready to share with Izz, lest he scare her away.

He was interrupted from his dressing by a knock at the door. "Mr. Cadian," a short, round woman said from the other side. Cade opened the door and peered down at Cynthia Clark, or Lady Cynthia as she was called during the show. The older woman ran one of the ticket counters up front, or the merchandise stand when needed. She insisted on calling him by his full last name, for reasons he still couldn't figure out. "There is a young lady here to see you."

"Tell her the knights are practicing. We can talk after the show at the meet and greet," he answered, not the least bit interested in seeing which *young lady* had come calling. They all had their fair share of fans wanting to get a little extra before or after the show.

"She's quite insistent, Mr. Cadian. Says she knows you."

"They always say that, Cynthia."

The older woman smiled, a twinkle in her eye causing him to frown. "She also says you have a bet to settle, and she's not leaving until she gets what she wants."

Surprise had him pausing, satisfaction turning his frown into a cautious smile. He didn't even hear Cynthia chuckle as he brushed past her and headed for the large wooden drawbridge-style doors up front.

Cade opened the side door just enough to slip through, in case a crowd had already formed. The sidewalk was empty, save for the one lone figure leaning up against the railing, staring out at the pond with a wistful yet nervous expression.

"You called, m'lady?" he said in his best charming accent. Izz glanced over her shoulder at him and he felt his stomach clutch. The woman was too damn beautiful for her own good, and he doubted she even knew it.

Izz pushed herself off the railing. "I brought you your clothes back," she said, gesturing to the bag in her hands.

Disappointed, Cade accepted the bag. "I don't have

yours with me, though I'd be happy to give you another tour of my home should you want them back."

Smooth, too smooth. She ignored the smirk playing at the corners of his far-too-attractive lips. "And I've come to collect on my bet."

"Oh?" Cade leaned against the door, curious. "And what are your demands?"

"I want the VIP tour. Of this place," she continued, gesturing to the building when Cade merely stood there and stared at her. "I want to see how it all works."

His dark eyes roved over her, at her tight jeans, fitted black tank top, flip-flops. Hardly the attire for a knight's lady. "Why?"

"Why not?"

They stared at one another for a moment, a silent challenge, before Cade relented. "A bet is a bet, m'lady," he said as he offered her his arm. Not surprisingly, she ignored the gesture and entered the building. "This way."

She followed him inside, past the entryway she'd seen once before, and through a side door. While she'd already seen everything the outside had to offer, the inside proved much more to her liking. They passed a few office areas, explored a room that held an enormous array of costumes, then approached the locker rooms. Izz glanced in one door as it opened to see that it looked like any other changing area, with metal lockers and benches. Farther down the hall, though, was the weapons room.

He gave her a tour of that room, showing off the various swords and battle axes. "All forged in modern-day smiths out of titanium. They are completely real, and completely sharp. Just don't touch anything. Company liability and all."

She was impressed, but tried not to show it. Cade watched her take it all in, then glanced away to double check a weapon. When he looked back, she was holding a smaller dagger. "You're not one much for listening, are you?"

Caught, Izz sent him a sheepish grin. "Maybe I just like to be contrary."

"That much is obvious."

Unable to help herself, she performed a quick spin and threw the blade at a target on the far wall, hitting it almost dead center. Cade whistled, not afraid to show that he was impressed, then retrieved the weapon.

"Where'd you learn that?"

"My father," was all she said in return.

Leaving the room, Cade led Izz around to the other side, where the stables were housed, half indoors and half leading outside. She looked on at the mass of people caring for the horses, brushing them down, braiding their manes, feeding them. It was a flurry of organized activity, and she could appreciate the intricacies that were so perfectly orchestrated within a relatively tight space, considering the amount of horses and people.

"And the place you've seen before but never from this awesome angle," Cade said as he led her through a dark hallway, "the arena! My favorite area of the whole building."

Izz stepped out from behind a thin curtain and stopped on the edge of the arena, taking in the scene from the ground level. In the stands, no matter where guests were seated, there was always a downward angle. From this vantage point, she saw the world through the knights' eyes.

The lights were bright still, presumably so the few men and women milling about could prep the arena for the night's show. Two workers were securing weapons to a wall along the back of the arena, while a few more were coiling chains on either side that would be used to capture the villain in the center of the arena during the big finale. Two more were raking out the sand along the sidelines.

Izz walked to the center of the arena, vaguely aware of Cade following behind her, arms crossed casually as he watched her. She stopped in the middle and closed her eyes, taking in the scent of horses and sand, sweat and leather. She'd always loved the combination, an aroma that brought her imagination to a time she'd experienced only in the words she put to paper. Izz often wrote about warriors who risked their life to save the damsel in distress, though, more often than naught, said damsel ended up saving herself.

Women didn't depend on men in her stories.

As she stood there, eyes closed, mind soaking in the sensory details of this place, she began constructing a tale built of legend. Fiction, of course, but rooted in the truths her father used to tell her as bedtime stories. He'd always been passionate about history and loved to trace his family back as far as it could go, searching for some connection to the knights that lived in all his stories.

He'd died before he had a chance to find that connection. Even though she didn't really believe in stories of knights, Izz hoped to one day finish the work that had meant so much to him; whether it proved him right or her made no matter.

Eyes opening, Izz strode to the wall of weapons and ran a finger down a battle ax. With a gleam in her eye, she asked Cade, "You up for a duel?"

Brow furrowing, Cade uncrossed his arms and took a few steps closer. "Are you challenging me, m'lady?" Izz pulled a staff from the wall, figuring it was a safer bet than one of the huge swords she likely couldn't lift, and dropped into a fighter's stance. Cade only stared at her. "Why?"

"Because I won the bet and get whatever I want."

"And you wish to fight me?"

Izz never dropped her stance as she replied, "Where is your sense of adventure, Knight Cadian?"

With a grin that matched the challenge in her eyes, Cade yanked an identical staff from the wall and began to circle her. She watched him carefully, so intently and so eagerly that he was nearly unnerved. He had a fleeting thought that perhaps she actually knew what she was doing, then brushed it off as a foolish notion.

"I'll go easy on you, m'lady."

Izz twirled the staff in one fluid motion. "As will I."

They launched into battle, staffs clanging against one another in perfect unison, each blocking and defending as though they'd been sparring together all their lives. Sand kicked up as Izz leapt back, narrowly avoiding a staff end to the gut. Cade advanced until her back nearly hit the wall. Not to be deterred, Izz fell to her knees and tumbled out of the way. When she leapt back to her feet, she saw the look of surprise spread across his face.

"My father taught me well," she informed him, the staff arcing as she flicked her wrist.

"As did mine," Cade replied, moving so fast that Izz barely had time to defend herself. He lashed out with the staff and she arched backward, avoiding the hit but also forced to break her stare. That distraction was all Cade needed to take the advantage, swiping the staff across her ankles and flipping her on her back.

Shouts rang out as she fell, the other knights cheering on their friend as he stood over her, staff pointed at her throat. "Never take your eyes off the enemy, m'lady," he warned, staring down at her. When their eyes locked, the fierce expression on his face softened, as did his stance. Izz offered him a smile and, when he returned it while offering her his hand, took that second to shift her body and arch her back, wrapping her legs around his waist and twisting them both so that he was now on his back and she was straddling his hips.

"Never let down your guard when the enemy smiles at you, good sir," she mocked to the sound of catcalls and laughter.

Cade stared up at her. "If this is losing, then I'd rather get used to it."

It was then she noticed his hands gripping her thighs, his knees pulled up and bracing her from behind. Suddenly uncomfortable, and a little embarrassed, Izz jumped up. "Consider the bet settled," she said, brushing sand from her hands and legs. "I have to go anyway."

Cade rose and handed the staff to one of the workers, who started prepping the arena again with a slight grumble. "I'll walk you out." They walked silently, side by side, to one of the many 'employees only' doors that opened to the main square. Just before opening it, Cade paused. "What are your plans tonight, my Isabella?"

She turned a smirk up at him, not bothering to correct him on her name. "Cheering on my favorite knight, of course."

"And who might that be?"

"Don't know." She shrugged playfully. "Don't know where I'm sitting yet."

He grinned after her when she flounced through the door, sand still covering her back.

Chapter 11

THEY DONNED YELLOW SASHES THAT evening, cheering for handsome and blonde Knight Rowan instead of dark and mysterious Cade, who had taken his turn as the villain for the night's show. Izz didn't miss the not-so-subtle glances in her direction, the winks just before he did something particularly dangerous. Her friends laughed and nudged her with their shoulders, encouraging her to give some sort of response other than a smile, but Izz kept her reaction calm and collected. After all, she was leaving in a few days, and this whole trip would be but a momentary aberration from her life of melancholy and lost memories.

Despite her resolve, her breath caught in her throat during the final battle as she watched Cade fight with Rowan. Their dance of ax and sword mesmerized her, sand kicking up as they flew across the arena, ducking and rolling and spinning so fast she was nearly dizzy. Even though she knew the knight always won, a part of her silently rooted for Cade.

The crowd erupted into cheers when Rowan rushed forward and spun Cade around in an intricate tumble, kicking him in the back while arcing up with the sword. The metal cut into the fabric at Cade's shoulder and ripped a hole the size of her fist. She couldn't tell if blood had been shed from her distance, but Izz clutched her hands together in worry. She knew accidents were common in their fights, and knew Cade could take care of himself, but, damn it, she wanted to run out there and make sure he was okay.

The show ended soon after, Cade soldiering through the fight like the warrior he was, defeated by the knight in shining armor that had most of the women in the crowd weak at the knees. Izz had to admit that his fair-haired complexion and strong face matched by a damn sexy accent were a dangerous combination – though one that did nothing for her.

She followed her friends into the lobby after the show, determined to avoid Cade and another forced date. Sure, she'd enjoyed her tour of *Quest* and her mock fight with him, but that was as far as it could ever go.

Izz saw him across the room posing with a group of women. Being the villain, he kept his expression severe, yet with a hint of humor that she found somewhat adorable. Her eyes crinkled slightly at the corners as she watched, then narrowed when she saw one of those women, a gorgeous redhead with legs for miles, turn her grin up to Cade and whisper something in his ear – at the same time that her hand slipped something in his pocket.

From her spot in the corner of the room, she watched the scene play out, arms crossed and eyes all but shooting daggers at the woman. Cade grinned at what Izz guessed was a very open invitation, then whispered something back that had the woman's sultry smile turning into a pout, then a glower when that failed to garner the response she wanted. As she turned around and walked away, Cade reached into his pocket and retrieved the paper, tossing it in a trash can behind him.

Relief filled Izz, relief mixed with confusion and annoyance when she realized she was actually jealous. *You have no right to be jealous*, she told herself, taking in a deep breath. *He's not yours. You can't have that again.*

But she wanted it. Shit, how she wanted it.

In that moment Izz realized just how lonely she was, just how much it hurt knowing she was soon to return to an empty home with no one to share her life with. And, in that loneliness, she recognized the despair that came with it, the guilt in *wanting* someone to be there, when it couldn't be the one she'd vowed to love forever.

Pushing herself off the wall, Izz headed for the door, not bothering to find her friends, who she was sure were mingling with the knights, looking for some sort of trouble to get into. Deanna had her eye on one of them since their first trip, and was likely securing herself a date after their trip through the haunted house.

The salty air welcomed her as she exited, wrapping her in a warm embrace that led her down to the beach across the street. Izz walked along the shore as close as she could without getting her feet wet, enjoying the feel of damp sand beneath her toes. It was different here, on the east versus the west coast, but she almost felt at home.

Almost.

Izz walked down the shoreline for almost two hours, breathing in the salt air, peering through the darkness at the leftover sandcastles and footprints and artwork that had been created earlier in the day. She passed a few couples going for a stroll hand in hand, and eventually sat down on the sand, lying back to stare up at the stars. For once she didn't want to think, so she forced her mind to clear, focusing only on the stars and the light they shone down on her.

When her phone beeped, she checked to find an urgent text from Olivia, panicking over her disappearance. Izz sent back a quick message to let her friends know she was fine and to head back to the hotel without her, then went back to her musings about nothing at all.

Soon, all too soon, her mind turned to Cade. Try as she might, she couldn't push his face from her thoughts. Determination built within her. Izz pushed herself up from the sand and brushed herself off, then began the long walk down the beach. She vaguely remembered what the house she was searching for looked like, and when she came upon the back deck, knew she was right. The large glass door that opened onto the deck gave her a clear view into one of the back rooms, light glinting off the swords hanging on the wall.

Steeling her nerves, and pushing down the guilt threatening to turn her feet away, Izz strode up the back steps and knocked on the glass door. For a few minutes, she stood there silently, wondering if he was even home, before she realized there was a good chance he wasn't alone. She'd nearly changed her mind when she saw Cade coming down the stairs wearing a pair of dark-blue sweats and a faded white shirt.

"Lady Isabella," he said with a small smile after opening the door. "To what do I owe the pleasure of your visit?"

Izz lifted a shoulder, suddenly wondering why the hell she was even there. "I just figured … You know what? I'm sorry, it was rude of me to show up unannounced. You were probably busy."

"Hey." He caught her by the arm before she could turn away, having interpreted her meaning beneath those few words. "I'm not busy. I just got out of the shower, had to get dressed first. Come on in, m'lady."

His ability to switch from regular guy to knight and back again both charmed and annoyed her. Izz entered slowly, suddenly unsure of why she was there. He must have sensed her hesitation, because he asked, "Can I get you something to drink? Water, Coke, wine…"

"Wine is fine," she answered absently, needing a drink to take the edge off. She followed him to the kitchen, figuring that was a safe place to talk. Neutral ground for the knight and his damsel in distress. The thought made her snort, which earned a curious glance from Cade.

He is too damn good-looking for his own good, she thought as she accepted the glass of red wine he placed in her hand.

"To quench your thirst, m'lady."

Izz sighed. "No offense, but can you drop the knight speak for a night? Just talk to me like I'm a regular person."

Cade observed her from his place across the counter, for long enough that she wasn't sure what he would say next. When his shoulders relaxed, so did she. "What happened to you earlier? I saw your friends, but they said you disappeared. I was worried."

"Just needed some air," Izz replied, taking a sip of wine. She wasn't much of a wine drinker, but even she could tell this one was expensive. "Too much going on in my head, I guess."

"Do you want to talk about it?"

"No."

After a pause, Cade asked, "Then what do you want? Why did you come over, Isabella?"

Izz sighed and ran a hand through her hair. Picking up the glass of wine, she paced ever so slightly, taking in everything from the pictures of who she guessed was family on the fridge to the intricate handles on the cabinets. "I don't know. I want ... I want ... Hell, you know what I really want?" When Cade only peered over at her, his expression welcoming her to continue, she gave the answer she knew was completely ridiculous. "I want to sit on the couch and watch a movie and just hang out and not talk about what's going on in my head."

She didn't admit to the rest of it, that she wanted one night to feel somewhat normal again, to sit next to a man on the couch and get lost in a movie and just not have to worry about talking or feeling.

As if he could read her thoughts, Cade simply nodded and gestured with his head. "Then a movie it is. The lady's choice."

While she browsed the large entertainment center filled with movies, Cade watched her carefully. He couldn't figure out why she was there, why she'd run from *Quest* to who knew where, only to show up on his back doorstep with no real agenda other than watching a movie.

There was more to the story, he knew, but something was holding her back from being honest. He wouldn't push her, or ask for her undivided trust, given that he'd known her for all of three days. But those three days were all he needed to know he wasn't letting this one get away so easily. So he'd let her go through whatever this was, and wait for her to come to him.

When she finally selected a movie, Cade was relieved to see that she'd chosen an action flick rather than one of the romantic comedies his sister insisted on shelving 'just in case' he happened to be entertaining a lady friend, as she called them. He was surprised when she sat down next to him, as he'd assumed she would take the chair to be by herself.

Izz picked up the remote sitting on the coffee table and stared at it for a few seconds before handing it to him. "I have no idea how to work this alien remote. Have at it."

Cade chuckled and took the remote, pressing a few buttons to get the movie playing. At the same time, the lights dimmed. "Can't watch a movie with the lights glaring in your eyes," he explained when Izz looked over at him, one brow raised.

Smooth, too smooth. But she didn't say anything, instead settling back against the plush cushions and focusing on the television. Cade refilled their glasses before doing the same.

Chapter 12

THEY WATCHED THE MOVIE IN silence, stirring only when the credits rolled at the end. Rising slowly, Cade looked down at Izz, somewhat surprised to see that she was still wide awake, albeit a bit flushed from the wine. "Next?"

"Gentleman's choice," she replied with the smallest of smiles.

Selecting a dark drama, Cade popped in the movie and took his place next to Izz, positioning himself a little closer this time. He offered her a blanket, which she accepted with a quiet thanks. Izz watched him out of the corner of her eye as he worked the weirdest remote she'd ever seen. The expression on his face was unreadable, relaxed but with a hint of something she couldn't identify.

The movie started with a melodramatic melody that she guessed was supposed to creep her out, but instead only made her sleepy. Fatigue, combined with the wine, had her head dropping to Cade's shoulder, and as she shifted to get comfortable, he reached over tentatively to take her hand in his.

This time, she let him.

Cade took a sip of wine and passed the glass to her, so she wouldn't have to move for her own, she guessed. They shared the glass, and one another's company, just like that, two relative strangers finding comfort in the dim lighting of a living room with a murder scene playing out on the screen in front of them.

She'd missed this, the feeling of comfort and security that came not from a man who could take care of her, as she could certainly take care of herself, but simply someone who wanted to be by her side for something as simple as watching a movie. By the time the film ended, she had no idea what happened, and was disappointed that she had to leave the warmth of the couch.

Cade stopped the movie, but didn't rise. Instead he looked over at Izz, who had lifted her head. "Up for another, m'lady?"

Izz yawned and straightened, her head spinning a bit. "I'm not sure I could stay awake, good sir," she answered sleepily. "My friends are probably freaking out anyway."

"They're fine. I texted Olivia to let her know we were watching a movie," Cade explained when Izz gave him a confused glare. "She gave me her number before we set up our first date. She was worried about you ... I wanted to make sure they knew you were okay ... Are you mad at me?"

His rambling sparked something inside her, an emotion she hadn't felt in a long time. He looked so concerned, so flustered, so innocently boyish, by her persistent stare that she began to giggle. She knew it was the wine, as she was most decidedly *not* a giggler, but couldn't stop it from escaping her now.

"You look so hand-in-the-cookie-jar scared," she

laughed out, amused even more by the look of confusion now spread across his face. "I can't … I can't even … That is the best look ever," she managed, unable to control herself as she pushed away from him, and nearly toppled over off the couch before he caught her, moving in a blur to wrap an arm around her back just before her head hit the coffee table and tugging her back up. Her laughter faded when he slowly pulled her against him, taking in his dark hooded eyes, the feel of his hand against her back.

"I've been waiting to hear you laugh just for me," he said softly. "It's a beautiful sound."

Izz wasn't entirely sure how to respond, so she didn't. Instead she kept her eyes locked on his, her breathing quickening, the rush in her head drowning out the thoughts telling her to run far, far away.

But she didn't run. Not when he pulled her on top of him, not when he tightened his hold around her back, not when he lifted his other hand to cup her cheek, thumb brushing across her lips.

"So beautiful," he murmured before bringing her mouth down to meet his.

She lost herself in his touch, her hands moving to grip his shoulders, her legs tightening around his hips as they pressed themselves together. A burning anticipation sparked within her, desire shaking her to the core. Her fingers moved to his hair, tugging lightly, but hard enough to produce a growl from him that had Izz deepening the kiss.

In one swift movement Cade lifted her from his lap and laid her down on the couch, covering her body with his own. His hands explored her stomach, her shoulders, her hips. Everywhere, she was electrified by his touch and a need built up within her that she hadn't felt in more than a year. She needed him closer, his hands on every inch of her. When his lips moved to her throat, her body responding in a way that stirred the same reaction from him, that need turned to panic.

Betrayal, her mind whispered, even as her body yearned for more.

Adulterer, her thoughts shouted against the pounding of her heart.

"Cade," Izz got out, her hands fisting in his shirt. "Cade, I can't." Her voice was quiet, so quiet that she wondered if they went unnoticed. When his lips dipped lower to her collarbone, Izz suppressed a groan. "Cade, I can't. My husband–"

The word, that single word she should have followed with an explanation, the word she hadn't really meant to say at all, cut off the moment like a bucket of ice-cold water thrown over them.

"Husband?" Cade repeated, lifting himself off Izz immediately. His face held a mixture of disbelief and confusion. "Did you just say *husband*?"

Izz swallowed hard, fighting back tears and the ache building in her chest. "Cade–"

"Don't *Cade* me," he interrupted, leaping to his feet and running his hands through his dark hair. His eyes flashed with anger and, she noted, pain. "You're married? I know I haven't known you all that long, but were you planning on telling me any time during our dates?"

A sigh fell past her lips, a sound of resignation tinged with annoyance. "You don't understand. I didn't mean–"

"You're right, I don't understand. I don't understand why you'd think I'm that kind of guy. I don't understand why your friends pushed you on me, and why you let them."

Her head snapped up at that, fury taking over guilt. "Excuse me? I wanted you to leave me alone. *You* wouldn't leave *me* alone."

"And yet you showed up on *my* doorstep tonight."

"Which was clearly a big fucking mistake." Izz threw the blanket at him and spun around, catching herself on the back of the couch when her head took a second to catch up with her body. "Consider me gone. Hey!" she yelled when Cade grabbed her arm.

"It's the middle of the night, Isabella. You don't have a car and you've had a lot to drink. You're staying." When he saw the fear mixed with irritation, he smirked. "Trust me, you and I will have nothing to do with one another tonight. I'll show you to the guest room."

He did just that, Izz too caught up in the whirlwind of wine, anger, and Cade's rapid change of heart to argue. She wanted to explain, and yet, something kept her from telling him, even though all it would take were a few simple words to remove the hitch in his voice and the hurt in his eyes.

By the time he brought her to the guest room and closed the door behind her without a word, Izz was too tired, and a little too drunk, to protest. She fell to the bed and wrapped herself in the blanket, clothes and all, letting the tears take her away to sleep.

THE SUN WAS BARELY BREAKING through the horizon when Cade opened his eyes the next morning. He'd tossed and turned most of the night, burdened by memories of having Isabella beneath him, her soft skin against his hands, those full lips whispering a secret that shattered an otherwise incredible moment.

Husband. She had a husband. He couldn't bear the thought of what came after that, so he'd cut her off, refusing to listen. He wasn't interested in hearing excuses, some plea of feeling neglected and unloved so she needed a fling to get through it all. So many of those women threw themselves at him and his friends at *Quest*, hoping for one night to forget it all and come home with a juicy story to tell their friends, but Izz hadn't struck him as that type, and he wondered how he didn't see it in the first place. He'd thought he found her, the one he was meant to be with, but it turned out to be a lie.

That hurt more than he'd expected it to.

With a sigh, Cade dragged himself out of bed and pulled on a pair of workout shorts, figuring he'd go for a run. He didn't have to work that night, so he might top off the exercise with a nap and a beer, something to help forget last night.

The guest room door was open when he walked by, the bed empty. Figuring Izz skipped out sometime early morning, Cade kept walking and was surprised to find her sitting on the back deck in one of the wooden chairs, feet propped up on the railing. He stopped, torn between telling her to go and pulling her into his arms. He wanted to hate her, but goddamn it if he didn't want to hear the sound of her voice one more time.

"I thought you left," he finally said, leaning against the railing, his back to the ocean. As hard as it was, he turned his eyes to her, seeing that her clothes from the previous night were rumpled and her hair was pulled back into a loose and messy braid.

"I almost left," she answered after a moment's hesitation. "But I figured I owed you an explanation." She dropped her feet and leaned forward, resting her elbows on her knees and lowering her eyes to the deck. "My husband," she paused, noting how he stiffened out of the corner of her eye, "my husband died ... over a year ago."

Of all the things she could have said, Cade hadn't been expecting that. All of the negative thoughts that had been stewing in his mind last night and this morning vanished, replaced by guilt for letting himself think so poorly of her. "Isabella–"

"Just ... wait." She held up a hand. "He got sick, and that ... that was it. It seemed like he was gone before we could even begin treatment. It was so fast, all those years together wiped away just like that and he was gone." A lone tear streaked down her cheek. "Eric died over a year ago and it's taken me this long to finally get out of the house, and the only reason that happened is because my friends basically dragged me out of the house." Izz stood and paced to the end of the deck, eyes trained on the water as she fought back tears. "Everyone kept saying I needed to get back to who I used to be. They said I wasn't the same person after I got married, that I settled down and wasn't as full of life because I wasn't as adventurous. But so what?"

She cast him a baleful glance before returning her attention to the sunrise. "I liked who I was with him. I liked feeling safe, and content, and unconditionally loved. And then ... I was alone." Sucking in a deep breath, Izz continued before she lost her nerve. "And now here I am attracted to another man who I just met and is the complete opposite of the one I married and all I can think is that I'm somehow betraying his memory. And I know that's stupid, because he's not here and never will be again, but I can't help it. I promised to love him forever. I'm not supposed to let myself love again. I don't know how to navigate this," she gestured to the two of them, "and part of me wants to just avoid it altogether."

When she fell silent, Cade took a step closer, then another when she didn't stop him. Finally he closed the gap between them and pulled her into his arms. He could sense the tears she was holding back, and wanted her to know it was okay to let them fall. "It's not stupid, Isabella," he whispered against her hair. "You are allowed to feel whatever you need to feel. I'm sorry if I pushed you, and for how I reacted last night. I should have let you explain."

"It's not your fault," Izz replied softly, her head resting against his shoulder. "It wasn't exactly the best thing to say mid-makeout." They both chuckled at that before she pulled away and wiped at her eyes. "And, on that dramatic note, I should probably head out."

"You don't have to go."

"I do," she insisted. "I need to change my clothes, take a shower, let my friends know I'm not dead."

"Pick you up in a few hours?" Cade smiled when her brow furrowed. "The guys and I are taking you and your friends out for the day. I think Josh, the blue knight from last night's show, has the hots for one of them. They seemed to hit it off at the meet and greet last night."

Disbelief swept through Izz. "Really? After everything that happened last night and what I just told you, you still want to go out? Why?"

"Why not?"

Izz held up a hand. "I just ... I mean, you barely

know me. Why put forth this kind of effort?"

Pressing a gentle kiss to her forehead, Cade took a step back and ran his hands down her arms. "There's something about you that has my attention, m'lady. Maybe it's your stubbornness." He kissed her cheek. "Or the way you suck at listening." His lips touched her other cheek. "Or maybe it's all that heart and soul beneath the tough-girl shell." Unable to resist, Cade brought his mouth to hers.

"So I'm going to see you again," he said after pulling away an inch. "And you're going to have fun, and give me more reasons to put forth the effort."

Izz huffed and stepped back, not sure what to do with the emotion spreading through her. With a small half-smile, she offered him a parting wave. "Until then, then."

Chapter 13

"WHERE THE HELL HAVE YOU been?" Deanna demanded as soon as Izz walked through the door.

"Morning, Mother," Izz replied, dropping her purse by the front door. "I texted you."

Deanna crossed her arms as Beth and Jackie came out of the bedroom dressed in similar yellow sundresses. "You spent the night with a guy you've known for three days. That's not like you, Izz. You're better than that."

"First of all, nothing happened, so you can stop mentally locking me in a chastity belt already. Second, get off my fucking back." Izz stalked into the master bedroom and slammed the door behind her. It was hard enough having revealed as much as she did to Cade, but to put up with the third degree from her friend was too much for one morning.

When Izz saw Olivia come out of the bathroom and lean against the door, she snapped, "What?"

The corners of Olivia's mouth quirked. "You sleep with him?"

"No."

"You want to?"

"…Yes."

"So why didn't you?"

Izz paused at the window, staring out at the morning crowd that was slowly starting to grow on the white-sand shores. "I told him about Eric."

The smile fell from Olivia's face, replaced by a concerned frown. "Really?"

"Not all of it," Izz sighed. "Just the fact that I had a husband and now I don't. It was the least I could do after … well … after."

"After a little morning makeout?" Olivia laughed when Izz turned her back on her. "Oh, come on. Lighten up, wild-woman-turned-prude. Good for you."

Izz let out a scornful snort. "Yeah, good for me. I freaked out mid-heavy petting and made it up to him by revealing a dead husband. He won't be looking for anything long term after that, I'm sure."

"Then he's not worth it," Olivia stated bluntly. "If he's a good guy, he'll wait. Who says you have to tell him everything all at once? And, for that matter, who says you have to tell him anything at all before you get under him?"

Izz threw a chair cushion at her friend. "I'm going to take a shower, horndog."

"Is he at least a good kisser?" Olivia asked as Izz passed her to go into the bathroom.

"Enough to almost get me under him," Izz replied with a wicked smirk before closing the door behind her.

CADE STAYED TRUE TO HIS word, picking up the girls at ten and treating them to breakfast before taking them to their first adventure of the day. He noticed that Izz stayed quiet for the most part, and he allowed her the time she needed to work through whatever emotions were battling inside her. But when her frown broke into a grin at the sight of their next destination, he silently patted himself on the back.

"Mini-golf?" Deanna asked incredulously. "I haven't done this since middle school."

"'Cuz you're boring," Olivia put in with a smirk, jabbing her friend in the ribs with a finger.

"Something tells me you'll find a reason to have fun," Izz said just loud enough for her friend to hear when she saw the two men walking up being them. Deanna looked over her shoulder at the knights from *Quest*, Rowan and Josh, a blush tinting her cheeks.

Looks like Josh isn't the only one with the hots for someone, Izz thought wryly, casting a glance over at Cade and wondering which one of her friends clued him in on the fact that her favorite pastime was mini-golf.

At the same moment, Cade was sending Olivia a silent thank you for her text that morning, letting him know just that.

They played a few holes, taking their time since the weekday meant there wasn't much of a crowd. Izz and Olivia proved to be the challengers, the other girls all but useless in even making par. The men enjoyed teasing them, though they were quick to tell them where to shove it.

"Hole in six!" Miley cheered for herself at the third hole, having shot her bright pink ball out of the rocks on the third swing. "Read those numbers and weep, boys." She laughed and high-fived Rowan, tossing back her wild mane of red hair in a way that was meant to be playfully seductive.

"Hole in six? Sounds like your life motto," Jackie taunted from the tee, eliciting snorts from the others. Miley just stuck her tongue out at her friend and shook her ass in her direction.

The guys hung back at the next hole, letting the girls go first. Most weren't the best of players, so Cade figured they'd be waiting a while before it was their turn. He chuckled when Jackie's ball sailed over the makeshift moat and landed in a bush, earning a round of jeers from her friends. His eyes focused on Izz as she pointed at her friend with her club and said something snarky, though he was too far away to hear what.

"So," Josh's voice cut into his thoughts, "a couple more days and they leave, right?"

After a moment, Cade tore his gaze away and glanced over at his friend of ten years. "So?"

"So, you seem awfully attached, is all."

Lifting a brow, Cade shifted so that his back was to the girls. "Aren't you the one who wanted to spend the day with Deanna?"

Josh laughed. "Yeah, but I'm fully aware she's going home. We have no illusions about a one- or two-night stand, if it comes to that. I just worry you're setting your-self up for disaster with that one." He gestured with his head to Izz. "You're putting in a lot of effort for someone who lives across the country."

Cade pushed back the irritation that was building in his gut. Before he could reply, Rowan spoke up from his right. "What are you going to do when she leaves?"

"Why do you care?" he snapped, not meaning to sound harsh, but the truth of their words biting into his heart. Already he regretted telling them what Izz had shared with him.

"It's just … Do you really want to always be in another man's shadow?" Rowan pushed, building off Josh's concerns. "I mean, I feel for the girl, and I know you said you'd give her time, but … doesn't it worry you, knowing she still loves a dead guy?"

As angry as it made him to hear his friends' words, Cade couldn't deny the edge of truth to them. He *did* wonder if he could live in another man's shadow, if it was worth the effort to even try. But, as he looked back over at the girls and saw Izz cheering for Olivia's hole-in-one, he knew that this girl would be worth anything.

Sensing eyes on her, Izz glanced over her shoulder to see Cade and his friends watching her carefully. Josh and Rowan looked almost wary, while Cade maintained that smooth, damn sexy smirk she'd come to know him for. For a moment she considered being weak at the knees before she pulled herself together and shook herself out of such foolish thoughts. After last night and this morning, she knew he was just humoring her until she left town. There was no way a man like him would stick it out with someone as broken as her.

Her attention was diverted from such thoughts by a buzzing in her pocket. She pulled out her cell phone and read the text message across the screen.

You look good today. Waiting to get my hands on you.

Izz smiled. She didn't recognize the number, but figured it was Cade giving her a compliment from only a few feet away. That guess changed when the next message came through.

He thinks he can have you. You are already mine.

Her smile faded quickly as her mind struggled to understand the message. Never having been one for secret admirers – sweet or crazy – Izz wasn't sure how to handle this one. So, she decided to ignore it altogether and slid her phone back in her pocket, just in time for Cade to join her at the tee before her turn.

"How about another wager, m'lady?" he asked, humor in his voice. "Allow me the chance to make up for my shortcomings in the haunted house. Best par for the last hole of the day is the winner. Terms named upon victory, of course."

Beth and Jackie giggled simultaneously, stopping only when Miley elbowed Beth in the ribs and shushed her with a not-so-quiet whisper. Izz lifted a shoulder in feigned boredom. Already the unease over her mysterious text had vanished, replaced by intrigue over the new bet. "If you insist on losing again," she answered.

Two hours later, Izz was standing back with her arms crossed as Cade sank a hole-in-one at the eighteenth hole – to her three-par score.

"Well, shit," she muttered to herself, tucking away her grimace in exchange for a small smile. Her friends razzed her while she held out her arms in Cade's direction. "So what's the damage?"

"Dinner and a walk on the beach this evening."

She eyed him suspiciously. "That's it?"

"That's it," he repeated, though his tone hinted at something far more than dinner and a walk. "Wear something fancy."

Chapter 14

IT WAS DARK WHEN CADE picked her up, the moon breaking through wispy gray clouds and the warm air blowing in lightly from the east. Izz ignored the catcalls from her friends as she stepped out in the only nice piece of clothing she'd brought to Myrtle Beach, a black dress that fell to her knees and showed off enough cleavage to make her mother blush, had she of been alive.

Cade offered her his arm and led her to his car, and for once she didn't ask where they were going. Nerves had set in, which seemed odd to her considering they'd been on a date already, and they'd had one hell of a makeout session. It didn't make sense to be nervous. He was just a guy her friends convinced to be nice to her, after all.

The car stopped at a small, intimate Mediterranean restaurant about a block from the beach. Cade stepped out, insisting she wait for him to open her door. Though she rolled her eyes, Izz conceded, and allowed him the opportunity to be a gentleman.

The hostess greeted Cade like an old friend, her eyes twinkling when she saw him walk through the door, and narrowing slightly when she saw Izz next to him. "The usual?" she asked Cade, ignoring Izz completely.

When he nodded, she wordlessly led them to a booth in the back and handed them both menus. After she had retreated back to the front, Izz turned her stare to Cade. "Come here often?"

"Once a week or so," he answered breezily. "The food is good, the atmosphere reminds me of home, and the owners are good friends of my parents."

"Home?" she pressed, curious as to his heritage.

"Knights, princesses, sword fights. We apparently come from a long line of nobles, with our roots tied back to the Middle Ages, back when dragons roamed the lands and honor was a way of life. Just the usual family heritage," Cade answered with a wink. He wondered at her reaction when she sat back with a curious, calculating expression, choosing not to answer his response.

The waiter interrupted his musings. "The usual, Mr. Cadian?"

"Yes, please," Cade answered. "And for the lady–"

"I'll have the Land Shawarma Salad to start, and the Moujadara entrée, please," Izz cut in. After the waiter walked away, she shot Cade a knowing smirk. "Don't let the blonde hair fool you. My father was Mediterranean. I know the cuisine well."

Yet another reason to make her mine, Cade thought with an amount of deep affection that nearly startled him. To take his mind off whatever was stirring inside of him, he asked, "So, what do you do? I realized earlier today that I never asked."

"I'm a writer," Izz answered, swirling her straw around in her drink. "Dark dramas and fantasies, mostly. I like stories that take place in worlds full of magic, where anything is possible. Most of them focus on some sort of battle and warfare based off pieces of history that interest me most, so basically a lot of knights and dragonslayer types. It's a lot of work, having to create new worlds basically from scratch, but I enjoy it. Readers seem to appreciate the detail as well. I make a good living off of it."

"That's amazing," Cade replied honestly. "What sparked your interest in fantasy and knights?"

Izz shrugged, eyes taking on a faraway glimmer as she thought about her past. "My father was fascinated by history, especially anything to do with knights. He was always talking about them, all these crazy prophecies. One of his favorite stories to tell was of this family way back in the day, when dragons lived alongside man, and knights were honored for their bravery in battle." She paused then, realizing just how much her words resembled the ones he spoke only moments ago. He encouraged her to continue with a brief nod.

"Um … Anyway, he would tell me of this epic battle between one man, 'emblazoned by the dragon's crest,' as he would say, who embarked on this grand adventure to save the woman he loved. She was the daughter of a nobleman, known as the most beautiful of maidens, he a brave knight known for his swordplay and courage on the battlefield. He fell in love with her for the way she embraced life, always looking for fun and adventure. They courted in secret, until they were exposed by the king's nephew, a man who dabbled in the dark arts and wanted the maiden for himself. His exposure set the course for a war between families that put all of their lives in the line of fire."

Cade swallowed hard. "Did … did he save her?"

Her eyes saddened. "No. The story doesn't have a happy ending. But my dad felt it had something important to do with our family, so he wanted me to be able to tell the story." Izz paused, going over everything she'd just said. "Well, this is great dinner conversation, huh?"

"It's fascinating," he answered honestly. "History was always my favorite subject. It's refreshing finding someone else who shares the same love."

"I don't think you found me so much as I was forced on you," Izz joked.

"Then I must remember to thank your friends."

In the dim, romantic atmosphere, Izz watched Cade carefully. She saw, and felt, the truth in his words, and even though she'd only known him a short while, she wanted to see and feel more.

They finished their meal with companionable conversation, talking about their families, parts of their pasts, plans for their future. He told her about his vision for *Quest* and franchising dreams, his hope to one day settle down. She told him about her life as a writer, and even a few details about Eric, feeling as though it was important to be upfront about such a serious past relationship. If it bothered him, he showed no sign.

By the end of dinner, Izz felt like they'd been friends their entire lives, and the trust she always said was so hard to find wrapped her in a cocoon of warmth as they left the restaurant and went for the walk on the beach that was his due.

He took her hand, kissing it as though he'd done so every night for years as they headed closer to the shore in the moonlight. After a bit they sat down on the sand, Cade positioning himself behind her. Izz settled back between his legs, against his chest, her head on his shoulder as he wrapped his arms around her stomach. Silently they stared out at the ocean, which was calm on this warm summer night.

"I'm not normally a basketcase," Izz said suddenly, not entirely sure where the affirmation came from. "I used to be a lot of fun. Life just … kind of took that away from me."

Cade was quiet for a moment before he replied. "I think you are plenty fun, m'lady."

"You don't know the Izz I used to be. The Izz I want to be and the one I try not to be today."

"Then change it. Starting right now."

Craning her neck to look behind her at the man observing her with such warmth, Izz frowned. "How?"

He gestured to the water with his head. "Well, let's start with the ocean … No one should be afraid of it. There is something so peaceful about the water, like you are one with the world. I want you to love it, to feel that."

He jumped to his feet, holding out a hand. "Come on, m'lady. It's time for a little fun. I will protect you."

Izz sucked in a deep breath, determined to get over her childish fear and not show just how hard it was. "And what makes you so sure you can cure my fear?"

Cade held his arms out to his sides in a cocky yet welcoming gesture. "I am your knight, m'lady."

With a small smile, Izz slid her hand into his and let him pull her to her feet. "Alright, then. Tonight, you be the knight, and I'll be your damsel."

Chapter 15

HE LED HER INTO THE sea, both of them fully clothed save for their shoes, until the water reached his ribs. Halfway out Izz started to shake, so he took her in his arms and carried her the rest of the way. Her fingers dug into his shoulders. At the same time, her feet kicked at the bottom until she was on her toes, and eventually she was simply holding on to him as he safeguarded her from all the things she was afraid of lurking in the ocean waters.

"See?" he whispered in her ear. "Nothing to be afraid of."

Izz had to admit she enjoyed the peace and quiet out in the water. The smell of salt surrounded her, the chill of the water a contrast to the warmth of Cade's body, the moon offering the perfect amount of white light to cast them in a glow all their own.

Giving in to the moment, Izz let the water glide her body in front of Cade. Her eyes staring intently into his, she lifted her legs until they were around his waist, her dress hiking up to her hips beneath the surface. Almost immediately his hands went to her thighs. Slowly, his eyes never leaving hers, those hands moved, sliding beneath her, fingers grazing wet skin. Despite the cold water, Izz felt the heat building between her legs, an ache for his fingers to slide just an inch closer.

As though feeding off her desire, Cade rubbed his thumbs over the thin fabric of her thong, resting his forehead against hers. She sensed the strain for control in his arms, saw it in the way he swallowed hard and closed his dark eyes, felt it in the gentle way his thumb massaged her center as it slipped beneath her pantyline.

Biting her bottom lip, Izz tightened her hold on his shirt and rocked her hips ever so slightly. The movement was enough for this thumb to slide into her fully. Cade grunted against her throat, the struggle for control growing tougher as he changed his hand's position and worked her with his thumb and finger until she was writhing against him, head buried in his shoulder.

Beneath the surface of the water, her legs clung to him, knees tightening around his hips, toes curling, teeth clamping down on her bottom lip as she let herself focus solely on the feel of his hand, hot against the sea. She felt one finger enter her, then two, caresses moving faster and faster in tune with the pressure rubbing circles against her clit.

He felt her release shudder through her body, just as she let out a muffled moan that might as well have been music to his lonely ears. For a moment they stayed locked in place, his hand only sliding away when her heartbeat slowly returned to normal. Placing that hand back on her thigh and kissing her lightly on the cheek, he asked, "Still afraid of the ocean, m'lady?"

Izz smiled, though he couldn't see it in the dark. So content was she in this moment that she didn't take the time to consider what just happened. "Consider me cured, my knight." Her reply was almost a purr.

He carried her out of the water, letting her drop to her feet and adjust her dress on the shore on somewhat shaky legs. Once she was steady again, he kept walking until they were at his house once more.

"Would you like to come in for a bit? I'll get you some non-ugly clothes to change into. Or we can walk back to the restaurant. The choice is yours, m'lady."

Hesitation racked her brain. Izz knew that if she went in that house, everything would change. She would be admitting to her attraction, and giving in to it at the same time. But if she walked away, she would once again be retreating back into that person she wished she hadn't become, and struggled daily to change.

Cade smiled when she took his outstretched hand, then led her up the stairs of the back deck. After unlocking the door, they stepped inside, into the safe space that was the kitchen. He made quick work of pouring two glasses of wine, then handed one to Izz.

"I'll get you something to change into," he told her, then jogged up the stairs.

While she waited, Izz wandered into the living room, taking in the swords and weaponry that were displayed proudly on the walls in an attempt to avoid thinking about Cade's fingers that had been inside her only moments ago. The pleasure of his touch still rippled through her. She didn't want to analyze what had been an incredible moment, so she let her body feel while locking negative thoughts out of her mind as she looked over the room.

One weapon she paid particular attention to, a dagger about the length of her forearm with a ruby-encrusted hilt that wrapped into the shape of a dragon, its tail curled around the wielder's wrist much like her own sword. Part of her longed to pull the weapon from the wall, but she kept her hands to herself, instead moving along. She hadn't taken the time to really look at them the first time she'd been in the room, and now found herself fascinated by the mix of swords and daggers, chains and spikes, and pieces she couldn't identify but wondered if they'd once been used to torture people. Izz stopped at one such piece, a thick metal ring with spikes pointing inward.

"Neck torture," Cade said from the doorway. Izz turned to see his arms full of clothes. "You clamp it around a person's throat and the spikes cut into the neck. Not enough to kill, but enough to … well, torture."

Izz lifted a brow. "Kinky," she said in jest.

"It was my grandfather's. He collected all sorts of weapons and instruments, claimed he was keeping in touch with our family legacy. He passed them on to me just before he died." Unsure how she really felt about the pieces, Cade held out his hands. "I wasn't sure what you'd want to wear, so … men's sweatpants and T-shirt, or stretchy, ruffly yellow dress?"

Eying her options, Izz reached for the men's clothes, then trotted off to the bathroom she'd used last time.

Cade stared after her, enjoying the way her wet clothes clung to her skin. When she stepped back into the room wearing his sweats and shirt, he swore his heart nearly stopped.

She was beautiful. So damn beautiful, with her ocean-swept hair a mess, her body hidden behind his large clothes, her feet bare. The woman could wear a garbage bag and still look incredible. There was a softness to her in

109

this moment that smoothed out the hard edges she'd built up around herself, a kind of cautious contentment that basked her in light.

Snapping himself out of his thoughts, Cade took her wet clothes and headed to the laundry room, tossing them in the dryer. "Shouldn't be more than a half hour or so," he told her, unsure how to proceed after their intimate moment. Izz nodded and continued her perusal at the wall, stopping at a pair of wooden swords. "For sparring," he told her when she glanced over her shoulder at him. That single short glance had his stomach doing all kinds of weird flips, but he kept his expression neutral.

She saw him try to hide the interest brewing in his eyes, and let him think he was succeeding. The truth was, though, that his stare was cutting deep into her resolve, enough so that she put down her wine and yanked a wooden sword off the wall. The second followed, which she tossed at him. Cade caught the sword easily, a frown forming on his handsome face.

Izz crouched into a stance her father had taught her in all their years of sword fighting. The move was a little awkward in the baggy borrowed clothes, but she managed. "Your move, good sir."

Cade stared at her, adorably bad ass in the oversized sweats and shirt, and twisted the weapon in his hand. It had been a while since he'd sparred with these swords, but the weight and feel were still familiar. His eyes narrowed as his frown twisted into a grin. "Have at it, m'lady."

Their advance was slow, almost seductive. The lengths of the swords grazed one another, the scratch of wood on wood the only sound in the room. Cade circled Izz, eyes trailing her body on one long gaze full of longing, so deep and intense that it left them both panting.

Izz stepped in and jabbed. Easily blocking the move, Cade wrapped an arm around her back, pushing her against the wall. Their bodies rocked together before she spun away and he gave chase, his sword reaching for her back, a move that she blocked with a skilled bend before leaping over the couch.

With a playful snarl he followed, catching her by the shoulder with one hand and turning her to face him. When the laugh died on her lips at the sight of his somber expression, he took advantage of the moment to knock the sword against the back of her knee, sending her to the floor.

In response, Izz leapt up and advanced, forcing Cade to back up until he hit the wall.

"Your move, hotshot," Izz growled good-naturedly, the tip of the wooden sword pointed at Cade's throat. If he felt any fear, or embarrassment, or caution, she thought absently, he certainly didn't show it. Instead they stared at one another in the dim lighting, only the sound of the ocean and their panting breath breaking the silence of that one single, long look. And then, just when Izz was about to drop her arm to ease the burn of muscle, Cade knocked away the sword and rushed her.

She'd expected a sneak attack, so when his lips captured hers in a frantic and passionate kiss, her mind momentarily blanked. Then the desire she'd been trying so hard to suppress kicked in and she kissed him back, both of them abandoning the swords in favor for one another's bodies. His hands went to her face and hair, tugging her against him; her hands went to his shoulders and chest, fisting in the thin fabric.

Cade pulled back long enough change the angle of the kiss, eliciting the quietest of moans from Izz. She breathed in the scent of him, sweat and salt and something darkly mysterious, allowing herself this one moment of weakness with a man who made her feel truly alive.

He spun her then, pressing Izz up against the wall, the metal swords clanging their protest against his assault. And assault he did, his mouth moving from her lips to her throat, feasting on the soft flesh there that tasted of the ocean. He felt her pulse, hard and fast, against his mouth, a sensation that nearly drove him mad. When her hands left his shoulders and gripped his waist, madness turned to frenzy.

Izz gasped when she was wrenched away from the wall, Cade's hands beneath her as he hoisted her up. Her legs wrapped around him almost involuntarily while her mouth found his again. In some deep, dark part of her mind, she knew where this would lead, the guilt that would be waiting for her in the morning. But she didn't care.

In this moment, she chose lust and life.

Cade cursed when his shoulder connected with the doorframe, earning a light chuckle from Izz. The low growl that formed in his throat turned that chuckle into a groan when he nipped at her bottom lip, starting the achingly slow ascent up the stairs.

Halfway through Cade stumbled, catching Izz before her back hit the stairs. But instead of picking her back up, he lowered them both, hips grinding into one another. Their mouths broke apart long enough for Cade to tear the shirt from her body, his hands cupping her breasts.

"So beautiful," he said quietly, eyes opening long enough to take in her bare torso. She felt his lips whisper down her throat, across her collarbone, sucking at the tender peaks until her breath came out in sharp gasps. He revered her breasts one at a time, massaging and licking, until she pulled him back up to kiss him deeply, yanking his own shirt over his head so they were skin to skin, heat pouring off them and wrapping them in a haze of lust. Izz could feel his excitement through the thin sweats, and suddenly she had to be closer.

Now.

When her hand slipped below the waistline of his jeans, Cade's breath caught and his hands clenched into fists. Her slender fingers wrapped around him with enough pressure to spur his hips into action as he rocked against her touch.

"Fuck," he whispered against her lips, bracing himself on his knees. "Isabella … upstairs."

With that he slid one arm around her back and the other under her ass, lifting them both off the stairs. She continued to torture him, unbuttoning his jeans for better access and stroking him until he was weak in the knees. He barely made it to the bed before he dropped her to the mattress, following her down.

When Izz started to push down his jeans, Cade stopped her. "My turn," he told her with a wicked grin, lowering himself to her smooth body, kissing a trail from her mouth to her breasts to her stomach, allowing her the time to anticipate what came next. She was so lost in the sensation that she didn't even feel his fingers at the hem of her pants or the tug of them leaving her body. Only when she lay before him naked, body nearly quivering with want and need, did nerves set in.

"My move, m'lady." Cade shook his head when she

113

made to cover herself. He grabbed one ankle and tugged her downward until her butt was at the edge of the bed, then positioned himself between her legs.

"I believe I won the battle," Izz managed to reply, not yet willing to give in so easily. She gazed up at Cade, who hovered over her just out of reach.

"Then allow me to give you your reward," he said with an impish grin, his hand trailing down her stomach, fingers stopping at the soft flesh just below.

"Cade–" Izz started, her words ending on a whimper when his fingers pressed harder, sliding between the wet folds, entering her one, two at a time, his thumb rubbing circles at her core. Then his mouth joined his hand, the warmth of his breath and scruff of his jaw adding to the intensity, bundling in a swirl of desire between her legs. Her fingers wrapped around his long black hair, pulling him closer to her as his tongue flicked against her clit in a fast and rhythmic dance of heat.

A sharp buzzing sensation built, slowly at first, heating her body from the inside out, quaking in her legs until she didn't think she could take it any longer. It had been long, so long, a time since anyone had touched her, since a man had treated her body with such gentle yet persistent admiration, that she had to fight back the tears – just as she stopped fighting the pleasure that ripped through her.

She cried out his name, a short, gasping syllable that brought his mouth back to hers. Her hands pushed back his jeans and he removed his own from her body long enough to help. At the sight of her blue eyes looking him up and down, mouth parting and tongue licking her lips when her stare lingered at the part of him throbbing, aching, for her most, Cade couldn't hold back any longer.

Her legs slid around his waist as Cade positioned himself, kissing her at the same time as he slid inside. Izz bit back a gasp in favor of his kiss, lifting her hips to meet his as he slowly thrust into her, skimming his hand between them until he was once again teasing her both inside and out. He tried to hold back, afraid of hurting her, but so hard by the feel of her slick heat that he nearly lost control.

"Cade," Izz breathed against his lips, lost in the feel of her body so full of him, "harder."

That was all the cue he needed, ready to follow her every want and demand, thrusting against her faster, harder, the thud of the headboard against the wall singing the rhythm of their oblivion. Izz gave in to herself and her emotions, nails latching on to his back. Cade lost himself in the scent and sound of her, burying his head in the crook of her neck. They built the sensation of heat and passion, their cries cutting through the night air, circling back to surround them in a cocoon of frenzied safety as their walls fell down together.

Chapter 16

HER BODY FULLY SATED, IZZ allowed Cade to pull her against him, nestling in the crook of his shoulder while she caught her breath. Their legs intertwined, bodies slick with sweat, his hand resting gently on her waist. They laid like that in companionable silence, enjoying one another's company and the fresh memories of intimacy.

"How does it end?" Cade's soft voice drifted into her fuzzy subconscious. Izz stirred slightly, not realizing she'd almost fallen asleep in his arms. "The story about the knights?"

It took her a moment to remember what he was talking about. "Oh … Well, the knight and his maiden were courting in secret, falling in love a little more with each passing evening spent beneath the stars. When they were exposed, they considered fleeing, but the knight knew his honor would forever be in question should he leave. But staying meant his maiden was vulnerable, and soon she was captured by the king's nephew, after he murdered her entire family right in front of her."

Izz paused to take a long breath, remembering lying in bed as a child, listening to her father's deep voice telling the fairy tale she'd loved most. "The knight went through battle and bloodshed for his damsel, fighting the dark arts and risking his life countless times. Finally, after weeks of searching for her and the king's nephew, who had disappeared as though made of air himself, he found her atop a cliff in chains, beaten and broken in the worst possible ways. It was said that the chains wrapped around her arms and anchored to the ground at her sides so tightly that should she move, her shoulders would dislodge.

"He ran for her, desperate to save her, but as he came closer the wielder of the dark arts appeared, and there, atop the hill, they fought their final battle. At some point, the chains broke free, whether by the force of an errant sword stroke or magic, it was never revealed. The knight struck down his enemy and turned to celebrate his victory, but when he looked into his maiden's eyes, he knew then that he had already lost, that *she* was lost. What her captor had done to her in those lost weeks, to the ones she loved, had broken her. The knight came closer, tried to save her, to speak to her wherever she had retreated inside herself, but just before he could touch her, she jumped."

Izz adjusted her head, soothed by the even beat of his heart despite the sadness of the story. "The knight couldn't accept her death, and traveled far and wide to find someone who could bring her back. Finally he found an old woman revered for her gifts in magic who told him that, while she couldn't bring back the dead, she could promise a future where their spirits celebrated together, where one man and one woman would be reunited as one soul.

"The knight agreed and the woman worked her magic, but all magic comes with a price. For the knight, that price was the memory of his beloved. For the rest of his life he would remember the feel of her, her scent, that empty sensation of being without his other half, but never would he see her face or hear her voice, or remember what they shared together. Those memories she worked into her magic, casting it into the earth.

"To the maiden's family, what was left of them, she gave a sword, the same sword the knight had used to so valiantly fight for her life. To the knight she gave a wooden box, and in that box was a prophecy, which held but the promise of a future in the form of a trinket. Only the son of his son's son would be able to open the box and foretell the fate the old woman had bestowed upon his family, and only he would know what that trinket was, though he would not know why it was significant. The knight was forced to marry and bear children if only to complete the prophecy, knowing he would die before it was revealed. He never quite knew what the box promised, not being able to remember the maiden he lost, only that he was giving his descendants a chance at the happiness he'd once known and could still feel as a wisp of breath in his heart."

Izz took in a deep breath, forgetting how much she'd missed hearing her father tell the story. "It is said that the maiden's family tried to deceive the knight, as they were angry with him for his failure. They didn't want another to go through the pain of loss as they did, and so they gave away the sword and stole the box, and it was never seen again. Some suspect it fell into the hands of the king's nephew. Others still insist that the knight never let the box out of his possession, and that both families stayed the course, hoping for the day their loved ones would be together again.

"But all stories agree on one thing. When the box was

finally opened, the prophecy foretold of three souls meeting in the far, distant future. A man of courage and power, a woman of bravery and wildness, and the evil that would try to tear them apart. When they met, either two would survive in the light of good, or one would live in the shadow of darkness. For good to triumph, the two pieces of the prophecy must be reunited. For evil to claim its victory, they would have to be destroyed."

When she fell silent, Cade asked the one question at the forefront of his mind. "And do you believe you are descended of them?"

"No," Izz answered lightly. "I used to ask my father that all the time. After all, why would he tell me the story over and over again and care so much about history if we weren't? But he would never tell me what became of the prophecy. He said that we made our own fate, and that no matter where we came from, our lives were what we choose it to be. It's just as well. I write fantasy, but I don't believe it."

"No?"

"No," she affirmed. "There's no such thing as ages-old prophecies and magic boxes that foretell the future. It's a nice thought, but I prefer to believe I'm in control of my life."

Izz didn't allow her thoughts to turn dark, to all the things she *couldn't* control and lost as a result, instead enjoying this moment with a man who made her feel parts of herself she'd forgotten even existed. It almost frightened her, how comfortable she felt in his bed, how perfectly they fit against and within one another, as though molded of the same stone.

That thought had her pulling away and excusing herself to the bathroom. She felt his eyes on her as she crossed the bedroom, not trying to hide her naked form. Nervous as she may have been, she wasn't shy about her body and took pride in how she looked. By the time she came out of the bathroom, Cade had propped an arm behind his head, waiting for her to come back to him.

As she strolled back to the bed, biting back a smirk, she took a second to look him over. The sheet was pulled up to his waist, covering his lower half, but his upper half was certainly one hell of a sight. His days as a knight had been kind to him, crafting a body of hard lines and broad muscle. Always an arm girl, Izz let her gaze linger over his biceps and shoulders before drifting it down his chest and stomach. Traces of black ink curled around his right bicep, and she realized she'd never actually seen his back – perhaps because she was so content being on hers last night.

She bit back a confused frown when he shifted and scooted to the end of the bed, effectively uncovering himself as he sat before her. Though Izz had never been one to back away from a good-looking man, the sight of him ready for her nearly made her blush, especially when she remembered just how well he knew how to work with what he had. He wasn't shy about his desire, using one hand to readjust and tug at himself in a move so goddamn alpha male that she nearly licked her lips.

"What are you doing?" she finally asked as he pulled her between his legs, fingers sliding behind her.

"Stand still."

She bristled at the command. "Why?"

"Because I said so." Cade's grip tightened and she positioned her hands on his broad shoulders. Before she could try to push away, he pressed a kiss to her stomach.

"I want to look at you," he said, his voice thick. "Every part of you."

And look he did, his gaze followed by his touch as he took in every inch of her body as though committing it to memory. Izz let him touch where he pleased, enjoying the mix of warmth and tingling that worked through her body. She could have felt exposed, but instead she felt worshipped.

"What's this?" he murmured when he turned her around and took in the dragon tattoo that traveled up her right side, the tail curling around her hip and the head arcing over her shoulder blade. He'd seen it when she walked to the bathroom, but she'd been too far away for him to truly study.

"A piece I got the day after I left home for good," Izz answered softly. "My dad was an artist. This was one of his drawings that I fell in love with as a kid."

"It's spectacular," Cade replied. And it was. Black lines twisted and turned into a strong dragon's body, accented with flecks of reds and greens that shimmered as scales. The dragon's tail swooped in toward its body, ending at a sharp point, and its head lifted up as though staring at the heavens. Broad wings curved mid-flight, accented with gold shimmers.

Izz felt him trace the tattoo from nose to tail. Most people, her friends included, had told her she was ruining her body getting a piece that big, that dark. Eric had always preferred she covered it up in public. But the way Cade responded to the art made her feel like some hidden part of her had known that one day he would be the one to look upon it, like no other woman in the world would ever compare.

"Cade!" she laughed when he moved quickly and pulled her down until she was on her back and he was on top of her. The laugh died on her lips at the somber expression in his eyes as he stared down at her.

"Stay with me." It wasn't an order, but a request. She heard the hope behind the words, a hope that kept her from immediately saying no. Though, she did have to resist the urge to squirm beneath the intensity of his gaze, and the desire in his words.

"You hardly know me," she said instead, her voice barely a whisper.

Cade leaned down and kissed her, fingers trailing in her hair. "I know you, Isabella. Stay with me."

This time she didn't say anything at all. Unable to form another argument, Izz wrapped her arms around him and let his embrace take her away.

Chapter 17

LATER THAT MORNING, THE PAIR walked back to the restaurant hand in hand to retrieve Cade's car, then he drove her back to the hotel.

"Will I see you tonight?" he asked as she slowly pulled herself from the vehicle.

Pausing, Izz ducked down and stared at Cade before shutting the door and leaning in through the open window. The expression on his face was sultry with a hint of hopeful, a sparkle in his dark eyes that had her wanting to jump back in the car and tell him to drive, wherever the road took them.

But, at the same time, the want to do just that scared the hell out of her.

"I don't know," she finally admitted. When his smirk turned into a suspicious frown and his brow furrowed, she was quick to correct herself. "The girls, I mean. We've hardly had any time alone together since we got here and I'd like to do something with them, just us, you know? We don't get to do this often."

That killer smile was back, along with a wink he sent her way. "Let me know, then. We aren't done yet, you and me."

Izz shot him a grin, waving as he pulled out of the parking lot and drove off. A pang of regret filled her chest as she wished she *had* gone with him, but knew she'd made the right call. While she was feeling a little frightened of her attraction for him, she really did want a day with her girls, despite the incredible night with one hell of a sexy man.

Her phone buzzed in her hand, indicating a text. Warily, Izz slid her thumb across the screen and frowned down at the message.

This changes nothing. Fate is coming.

"What the fuck are you talking about," she muttered, more annoyed than scared. She'd dealt with her fair share of weirdos, which was why eventually she'd taken on a penname, but there were always those who found their way around the mystery and tried to get under her skin – or worse. Each time, she dealt with them like she always did, which was always not the smartest way.

Fuck off, she texted back, leaving it at that short and bitchy reply before sliding the phone into her pocket.

Her friends were sitting around the table when she walked in, eating what looked to her like Beth's homemade French toast. "Yum," she said nonchalantly as she walked to the stove, feeling all eyes on her and having to bite back a laugh in the tense silence. Only after she'd loaded her plate and taken a seat at the end of the table did she lift her eyes to her friends, all of whom were looking at her in various stages of anticipation. "What?"

"You slept with him!" Miley shouted, a broad grin on her face. Her fiery red hair nearly fell into her food as she leaned in closer. "Tell me everything. Is he as hot underneath all those clothes as he looks?"

"Miley," Jackie admonished, just as her twin asked, "So how good is he with his hands?"

Chuckling, Izz swallowed a bite of French toast and answered, "I'm not going into detail with you weirdos. Suffice it to say, the man knows how to please." She dodged the rest of their questions while forking in another few bites, then noticed Deanna sitting quietly at the end of the table, arms crossed. "What's up, D?"

After a moment, Deanna unfolded her arms and pressed her hands on the table. "You don't even know this guy, Izz, and now you're screwing him? I thought you were better than that."

"Well fuck you too," Izz replied, more resigned than pissed. Deanna had always been the mother of the group, looking out for the girls any time a new man entered the picture. "Maybe now's the time to point out what a huge hypocrite you are, Deanna, seeing as how I'm pretty sure you're having yourself a good time with one of the knights. Or if you haven't already, you'll find a way to."

Deanna's arms crossed again. "Different situations, Izz. Neither one of us has any emotional attachment. You're leading a guy on just to feel better."

Izz rolled her eyes. "And here I thought you wanted me to move on with my life."

"I do, but not this way."

"Then *what* way?" she challenged. "What way should I move on that will make *you* happy? Because I'm pretty damn sure that after a *year* of wanting to follow Eric into the grave, *anything* would be better than going back to that!"

Fury building in her gut, Izz shoved away from the

table and stalked into the bedroom, slamming the door shut behind her. Through the door, she heard Olivia admonishing their friend. Words like "we came out here for Izz" and "what the fuck is your problem" met her ears before the door opened and Olivia slipped inside.

"Hey, girl."

"Olivia, I can't deal with any of you right now."

Her friend huffed. "Excuse me?"

"I don't need another round of essentially being called a whore."

"Good, because I wasn't going to call you a whore. I'm happy for you." Olivia nodded when Izz finally looked up. "Look, whether you never see him again or end up falling madly in love, I'm happy you're putting yourself out there. You deserve to feel special again."

"Glad someone thinks so."

"Were you safe?"

Izz regarded her friend with an impatient glare, but didn't reply since the answer was a resounding *no*. She couldn't get pregnant and Cade knew that, but they hadn't exactly gotten around to discussing other health concerns, though she preferred to think there was enough trust there to know the other was healthy.

Olivia turned around when her friend pulled out a bikini and started to change. "So," she continued, eyes on the wall, "all jokes aside about how hot I'm sure the sex was ... how are you doing?"

Tapping her friend on the shoulder to let her know she could turn back around, Izz took a minute to answer. "I'm having my moments," she replied honestly. "Last night, it was incredible, Olivia. And I don't just mean the sex. I mean how I felt with him. Like it was just us and there were no ghosts to haunt us. Then this morning I just … I got this feeling that I knew would come, that I really like this guy but am so incredibly guilty for feeling that way. And I know, I shouldn't feel that way, but I can't help it. It's something I need to find a way to overcome, but it isn't that easy."

A zipper sounded as Olivia pulled her own bathing suit from her bag and headed into the bathroom to change, leaving the door open a crack. "It will come, Izz. Don't feel like everything has to magically be better just because you rolled through the sheets with some guy. Some very hot guy," she added wryly.

The decision to add the next part ate at her until she knew she couldn't hold it back from her best friend. "Olivia … he asked me to stay."

At that the bathroom swung open and Olivia stood in the doorframe, dressed only in her bikini and an incredulous expression. "He … what?"

"He asked me to stay."

"With him? Like, hey girl I've only known for a few days and just had sex with, come be my forever lover?"

Izz laughed softly. "Something like that, yes."

"Do you want to stay?"

"…I don't know."

Picking up a couple towels and bottle of suntan lotion, Olivia dropped everything into a bag while she thought. "You know … the other day, not long before we left for Myrtle Beach, I had this dream. I'd had a bad day at work and wanted to blow off some steam at the bar or club, so I texted you to come hang out. But you texted back, 'Not today, Liv. I've got a man to get under.'" When Izz only shook her head, she continued. "I woke up laughing. Seriously! So now I challenge you to make this happen. Find the guy who takes priority over hanging out with your super-awesome best friend. Maybe it's Cade, maybe it's not. But you'll find him. I know it."

"Yeah, yeah." Wanting the conversation to end, Izz grabbed her friend by the arm and dragged her out of the apartment, ignoring the others cleaning up the breakfast dishes. They could catch up later. Right now, she needed time on the beach with her best friend.

JUST A FEW MILES AWAY, Cade stepped out of the shower and wrapped a towel around his hips, shaking water from his tousled hair. He entered the bedroom and glanced over at the bed, a grin quirking at the sight of the rumpled sheets, flashes of last night appearing in his mind's eye. He let himself remember the vision of her naked before him, the scent of her, the sounds she made when she was beneath him.

Cade shifted and shook his head, trying to think of something, anything else, when he felt his body responding to those thoughts. There was no denying he was completely, unexplainably, taken with this woman.

Dressing quickly in a pair of jeans, Cade sauntered into the living room and stared at the wall of swords until his gaze landed on the blank spot between two daggers. Only one sword would ever hang there, and he suspected, after so many generations of his family searching, that he finally knew who had it.

With that thought in mind, he walked over to that spot and ran his hand down the wall, the wood-grain design hiding the lines his fingers brushed over. With a gentle push the wall clicked and a panel drew back as a tray slid forward. On that tray sat a small wooden box crafted of intricate carvings that together formed a scene of intimacy. A dragon was etched into the left side, a sun on the right, a man and woman embracing in the center.

He ran his fingers over the dragon, a family crest, a symbol for cunning and craft in swordplay. It was a symbol he treasured deeply. Then he opened the box, as he'd done so many times to daydream of what once was and what could be. Inside, resting atop a velvet lining, was a necklace of black fabric and red stone. He didn't touch it, rarely did, but stared at it for a moment before gently closing the lid to take in the carvings once more.

"Come back," he whispered, fingers stopping when they touched the woman. "Come back to me, Isabella."

Chapter

18

FOR NEARLY AN HOUR THEY lay on the white sand, enjoying the feel of the hot sun, the sound of gulls and children playing, the crash of ocean swells just feet from their basking bodies. They didn't need to talk, their years of friendship allowing them the comfort of one another's presence without words.

Izz met Olivia when she was ten years old. Olivia had been the new girl in town, and latched on to Izz the second she found her hanging upside down from the monkey bars during recess. Their friendship grew out of races on the playground as kids to skipping class as teenagers to partying on the weekends as coeds. Everyone had come to know them for their tendency to leap before looking, and knew to call them first when looking for something wild and outrageous to do. They were the first to jump off the bridge with a bungee strapped to their ankles, the last to leave the white-water rapids in the middle of a tropical storm.

And now, they were two women with a lifetime of amazing memories who were perfectly content to just hang out as much as they were ready to paint the town red.

They met the twins on one of their many adventures as teenagers, goading them into trying their hand at surfing. Though reserved at heart, the twins took to Izz and Olivia, eager to be a part of the fun. Deanna came a couple years later, just after high school graduation, when she stumbled, literally, into them at a frat party and initiated a round of shots that ended with all three of them half naked in a random hotel pool. Izz could never really remember where Miley came from, just that she showed up one day and never left.

Together they made up an interesting group, six pieces of a whole that were bound together through thick and thin.

When rustling sounded beside her, Izz cracked an eye open to see Olivia rising, her spot taken by Deanna, who chose to sit on the towel facing the ocean, knees drawn up to her chest. With a sigh, Izz rose as well. "Look, D, if you're here to–"

"I'm here to apologize," Deanna cut in, looking over at her friend. There was truth in her eyes mixed with concern. "Look, I'm sorry, Izz. You're right, I'm a complete hypocrite and there is no excuse for what I said. I just … I'm afraid for you."

Though she wanted to be mad at her friend for a while longer, curiosity got the better of Izz. "Afraid of what?"

"That you'll get your heart broken again." Deanna cast a look in her direction, her eyes filled with regret. "You were so lost," she whispered, her voice breaking. "When Eric died, I thought you would die with him. We didn't know what to do or how to save you. Being out here has given me hope that the old Izz will come back to us.

And now you've met Cade, who is a great guy, but I'm just scared, you know? What if history repeats itself?"

Memories filtered into her thoughts, of the day she lost her husband, of the months that followed, of last night with Cade, all in a matter of seconds. Trying to overcome the sadness that started to wrap itself around her heart, Izz sighed. "Maybe it will, maybe it won't. I have no idea what the future holds. And maybe I will get my heart broken. But … I'm starting to think that maybe that's okay, since it means that at least my heart is working again."

After a moment, Deanna offered her friend a hug of peace. "You're right. I'm sorry I was such a bitch. Come brave the water?" She gestured and Izz shook her head, not willing to go in unless a certain knight was carrying her in. Deanna smiled, then joined the twins in the ocean. Izz watched them for a moment, remembering her own last venture into the waves, squirming a little when she remembered *all* of that venture. As if sensing her thoughts, a text came through, Cade's name flashing across the screen.

The knights wish to treat our ladies to a party on the beach tomorrow evening.

Izz smiled and texted back an affirmative, making a mental note to ask her friends though she was sure they'd be all for a beachside celebration.

"Hot knight putting that smile on your face?"

Izz squinted up at Olivia as she reclaimed her seat. "He wants to take us all to a beach party tomorrow night."

"Sounds fun to me!"

Before she could reply, another message came through, this one from an unknown number. Izz sighed as she read the text.

History will repeat itself. You won't escape me.

"Uh, did loverboy send that? Because it's super creepy," Olivia said, peering over her shoulder.

Knowing she was busted, Izz shook her head and closed the message. "No. Some creep has been texting me since I got here and keeps saying weird things about fate and history. Probably just another crazy fan."

"Or Bex," Olivia mused, then lifted a brow when her friend frowned. "What? The guy has had a thing for you for years. You know that. Hell, he made a move just before we left. He's a creep. I wouldn't put it past him to do this."

"Bex," Izz muttered, wondering why she hadn't thought of him before. Of course he would do something like this. She vowed to find him as soon as they got home, and set the bastard straight.

FOR THE NEXT TWO DAYS, Izz spent her time free of worry, putting her focus on rebuilding the friendships she had let fall to the wayside for far too long. She'd almost forgotten just how hilarious Beth and Jackie were with their twin act, how commanding Miley was within any environment, how much she valued Olivia and Deanna's words of advice regardless of whether or not she wanted to hear them. It had been too long, she decided, since they'd been together like this, and vowed to work harder on her relationships after the trip was over.

She wasn't sure how to define her relationship with Cade, and for now chose to ignore the question.

They dressed casually the night of the party. Deanna was already halfway to plastered by the time the guys picked them up, and eagerly latched herself on to Josh's arm when he offered to walk her down the beach.

"Ten bucks says they are found half naked with sand in painful places by the end of the night," Olivia said as the pair disappeared around a curve ahead of them.

"Twenty bucks fully naked," Beth and Jackie said at the same time, dissolving into giggles.

Izz shivered when Cade pressed a hand to her lower back, his palm warm against the thin cotton tank she wore over her bathing suit. A tingle ran up her back when he whispered in her ear, "Thirty bucks we show them up."

With a snort, she pushed at his side playfully, but didn't dispute him. Instead she let him lead them down the beach, the guys chatting about the previous night's show and the girls doing their best to sound as interested as they were.

The sun had lowered by the time they reached the party, a small section of beach with a large fire burning brightly, sending sparks of reds and oranges into the night sky. A large crowd had already formed, rowdy and ready to let loose. Music boomed from somewhere and drinks were set up close to the dunes, along with an array of chairs and makeshift benches.

Izz turned to ask her friends if they wanted a drink, but the twins had already disappeared. Olivia and Miley had latched on to one another and were scoping out the scene. Putting his arm around her, Cade led Izz around the fire, introducing her to a few of his friends. For once, she found it easy to talk to strangers, fitting in well with his crowd and feeling as welcome as an old friend with each new introduction.

After a while she stopped looking around for the girls, leaving them to their own devices for a bit. After all, they were all there to blow off some steam and just have fun. From somewhere on the other side of the fire she could hear Miley's laugh, and elsewhere heard Jackie yelling at Beth to stop taunting her with what was apparently a loaded water gun.

"Having fun?" Cade asked, kissing her cheek.

"Surprisingly, yes," Izz replied, accepting the can of Coke he handed her. It warmed her that he knew, in this situation, she wouldn't be comfortable drinking alcohol.

"I'd ask you to dance, but I'm not sure I could keep my hands off you."

"What makes you think I'd agree to a dance?" she deadpanned.

Cade squeezed her hip and was about to reply, but his attention was diverted, his eyes moving over her shoulder. She followed Cade's stare to see a young man, early twenties perhaps, holding a red cup and laughing in a group of men and women. He dressed like any other his age, in cargo shorts and a green cotton shirt that showed off his solid build nicely, but his looks told Izz why Cade was about to introduce himself.

The man's sandy-blond hair was long, past his shoulders, and curly enough to have her wondering if it was natural or salon made. His beard was impressive, thick and curled and extending a couple inches past his chin. For all intents and purposes, he looked like a modern-day knight, one Izz was sure would be a fan of the female show-goers with his broad chest and intriguing good looks.

She stood back and watched as Cade walked over, the other man introducing himself as Riley. Cade handed the man a card. "You've got a great look going here," he said, gesturing to the man's face. "We're always looking for

135

new knights at *Quest*, even just for the summer, and I think you'd fit right in, especially if you have any fighting or horseback riding experience."

Riley took the card and considered the offer, glancing back and forth from the card to Cade. "Sounds like fun," he finally said, pocketing the card. The two talked for a few more minutes, working out the details, before Cade returned to her.

As they walked away, finding a peaceful spot on the shore away from the beachgoers, Izz pushed at Cade with her shoulder. "So is this what you do? Go around picking up strange men off the beach?"

Cade chuckled. "Hey, when the look's right, it's right. Speaking of looks," he said as he tugged Izz against him, brushing his knuckles down her cheek. "Good evening, my delicate damsel."

A sarcastic laugh escaped before she could stop it. "I am neither delicate nor a damsel."

"I seem to remember you giving in to being my damsel not too long ago."

Her reply was cut off when he claimed her lips with his, a deep kiss that had her arching her back so that they were pressed together. Their tongues danced together in a foreshadowing of what could follow, were they not on a public beach surrounded by drunken partiers.

Breaking apart for breath, they laughed softly at their moment of passion reminiscent of teenagers sneaking away for a few minutes alone.

Cade began moving them slowly to the beat of a non-existent melody. "When do you leave?"

"Tomorrow night," Izz said on a sigh. Suddenly, California didn't seem so bright anymore. "We need to leave for the airport at four."

Cade took her in his arms, leaning his forehead against his. "Have you given any thought to my request?"

She didn't need to ask what he meant, but knowing what he wanted didn't make it any easier. "Cade … I don't … I can't … We barely know each other."

"You know that's not true. In real time, sure, but in what matters? You know we work."

What scared her was that she agreed with him. They *did* work, and she didn't know what to do with that. "It's not that easy."

"It could be."

Now getting annoyed, Izz untangled herself from his embrace and took a couple steps back. "Real life doesn't work like this, Cade. You want me to stay here in a strange place with a man I've known for all of one week, not even a week! And give up my entire life back home, for what? For a chance that it might work?"

"It *will* work."

"I'd like to believe that, but I know that even when you plan for everything to go perfectly, life can't wait to take it all away."

Cade closed the distance between them, sighing when she only stepped away again. "You're afraid of the worst, I get it. I really do. I understand that, with everything you've been through."

Shaking her head, Izz held up a hand. "You don't even know what–"

"Because you won't tell me!" he cut in. "And I'm not trying to push you. I'm just…" Frustrated, he ran a hand through his dark hair. "I'm trying to tell you that I–"

"Don't say it," Izz warned, tears brimming at the

words she was terrified of hearing again.

"I want you in my life, Isabella," he finished. "I won't say *it*, what you don't want me to say, because we both know it wouldn't be real. We haven't known each other long enough for that, and I won't pretend like we have. But I know that if you stay, we could get to that point that we say the thing we aren't supposed to say right now. I want you in my life, for as long as you'll have me."

They stood there staring at one another for a long moment, neither knowing how to end an impossible situation. Finally Izz shook her head. "I can't make this decision right now."

Cade swallowed hard and nodded. "And I can't watch you walk away."

So instead he walked away, offering her one last kiss on the cheek before turning around and disappearing into the night, down the beach in the direction of his home. The home he was offering to her as well.

For a long time after he left her sight, Izz sat on the shore watching the moonlight glisten off the smooth ocean waters. Tears rolled freely down her cheeks as she battled with emotions she couldn't quite identify.

It was completely moronic to consider staying with a man she'd known for less than a week, all the way across the country in a place she barely knew. It was foolish to put that much trust and faith in one person, in the idea of a relationship that may or may not work out. It was reckless to uproot her life as she knew it in favor of a dream. And yet, Izz wanted to be foolish. She wanted to be reckless.

She wanted to stay.

But that wasn't an option. She was an adult, not some fool-hardy girl in her early twenties who still thought *des-*

tiny was on her side. And staying would mean the one thing she wasn't ready to do – leave the house that had become a home with her late husband.

A sound behind her had Izz leaping to her feet. "Cade?" she asked, hoping he'd come back. What she would say to him, she had no idea, but longed to be in his presence nonetheless.

"Cade?" she said again when she heard nothing but the sound of footsteps through sand. An eerie sensation crawled up her spine. "Hello?" Turning in a circle, Izz peered through the darkness, seeing nothing but shadow against shadow in the dunes as the wind picked up, howling against her ears. She was sure the sound was amplified in her panic, but in this moment she couldn't distinguish fact from fear.

Putting as much bitterness and annoyance into her voice as possible, Izz shouted, "Okay, asshole! Enough is enough. Either come on out or get the fuck–ah!"

Izz sputtered when sand was flung in her eyes, wiping furiously as tears quickly built in defense against the gritty pain. She braced herself for an attack to come while she was blind, but surprisingly the beach went silent save for the waves breaking on the shore.

Once her vision was clear and she was sure she was alone, Izz allowed her body to relax, shoulders slumping just a bit as she tried to figure out what the hell just happened. Mystery text messager? Random psycho on the beach? Kid just wanting to have some fun? Freak windstorm? She never once considered it was Cade, but she did wonder if whatever just happened was a result of her being with him.

That thought in mind, Izz quickly made her way back

to her friends. Though she did inform them of her fight – if that's what it was – with Cade, she left out the rest. There was no need to concern them with the unknown.

Not yet, anyway.

Chapter 19

THE TRIP TO THE AIRPORT was quiet, one large SUV filled with luggage and women reminiscing on the good and bad times over the previous week. In the backseat, Olivia offered Izz comforting smiles and shoulder bumps. In the airport, she insisted on carrying most of her friend's luggage. Izz trailed behind them all, much like she had back in California, though this time she was constantly looking over her shoulder as though willing Cade to appear.

To do what? she asked herself. *Sweep you off your feet?*

Even if he did, she wasn't sure what her reaction would be. She wanted him to appear and ask her to stay again, but for some reason, she couldn't be sure she actually would say yes. All that would do was embarrass them both.

"He's not going to beg," Olivia said after she caught Izz looking toward the doors for the hundredth time.

"What?"

Olivia shrugged. "I'm just saying. He asked you twice to stay and you said no. He's not the type to beg."

"I'm aware of that," Izz said, bristling. "I just thought…"

"That he'd want to say goodbye to the woman he loves?"

Irritation flooded the sadness at her friend's words. "He can't love me, Liv. He's known me a week."

"So?"

Lifting a brow at her friend's nonchalance, Izz chose not to answer. Instead they passed through security without another word, Izz casting one last look at the front before she left everything behind.

EMPTINESS MET HER WHEN SHE walked in the front door. Not just silence, or the feel of a bare house after so long a vacation, but an emptiness that Izz felt deep in her heart. She dropped her bags at the door and wandered room to room, absently checking to make sure everything was alright but not really seeing anything. At some point she made it upstairs to her bedroom.

Not too long ago, she had shared this bedroom with another, a man she loved wholly. She came home to someone, someone came home to her. They shared a lot of laughs, arguments, good nights and bad, evenings curled up around one another and mornings rushing out the door after one last kiss. She'd taken advantage of those moments, thinking they would come one right after the other for the next fifty years, and learned all too harshly how quickly she could lose the things she cherished most.

For a while, the emptiness reminded her of Eric, and she'd held on to it, let it fill her until she was so hollow inside that she couldn't tell the difference between loneliness and happiness. But now it reminded her of Cade, and it felt wrong that her heart could so easily replace one man for another.

Feeling as though she were about to start some whiny inner monologue, Izz dropped onto the bed and forced her body into sleep.

HE STAYED HOME UNTIL HE Couldn't stand the silence any longer. Though he wasn't working for another couple days, Cade made his way to *Quest*, figuring a few hours spent with the horses would help clear his mind. The guys greeted him when he entered. They knew not to say anything, but the looks of concern on their faces nearly unnerved him. Worse were the sympathetic glances from Cynthia as he passed. Cade didn't know who told her, and what exactly was being spread around, but right now, he didn't care.

He wouldn't go after her. He wouldn't beg. He wouldn't ask her to love him. But, damn it, he would ache for her.

The horses greeted him with quiet whinnies, stretching their necks out to him in search of treats. He gave them each attention in turn until he reached his own stallion. "Good morning to you, too," Cade laughed when Starfire, his horse of six years, bumped his shoulder with his nose. Picking up a brush, he ran the bristles down his thick mane, feeding Starfire a few sugar cubes at the same time.

"Just you and me again, boy." Though he spoke quietly, it seemed that his words echoed through each stall and came back at him.

He'd never been one to feel alone. With a large family of two sisters and one brother, and countless aunts, uncles, and cousins around, Cade was blessed with loving company whenever he wanted it. His childhood had been a happy one of laughter and inside jokes and birthday parties that included the entire neighborhood. They hadn't had much, but it was enough for them, and they'd saved for years to get enough startup cash to open *Quest for Avalon*. Now it was a family business for a family that loved being together.

But for the first time in his life, he felt like something was missing. Unfortunately, he knew just what that was, and had no idea how to get it back.

He took his time in the stables. After a while, the tension in his shoulders started to ease and he felt a little less depressed. After cleaning up he headed back to the main room to check on things before the show.

"Mr. Cadian?" Cynthia approached timidly, her gray hair tied back in a tight bun at the nape of her neck. Later that hair would be curled around her shoulders. She handed him a slip of paper. "A young man called this morning, said his name was Riley. He said you wanted to talk to him about a job."

Cade took the paper. "I did. Thank you, Cynthia."

"Of course. And Mr. Cadian," Cynthia said when he made to leave. "She'll come back."

Cade paused, his back to her, her words striking him through the heart. Finally he turned and offered the older woman a sad smile. "Sometimes I'm not sure she was ever here at all."

Chapter

20

THE SUN WAS ALREADY CREEPING high into the sky when Izz finally crawled out of bed, shuffling in and out of the shower for the first time since arriving home three days ago. Though she'd never admit it aloud, her lazy tendencies showcased themselves more often than not when she was alone. Such was the life of a writer, she liked to think, having the freedom to lock herself in a room for days on end, TV on for background noise, mini-fridge stocked with sodas and table lined with her favorite snacks, not surfacing until the damn book was written already.

Her late husband had often teased her about her 'writer habits,' as he'd called them. Though he'd never intruded, he did let her know that he didn't approve of her tendency to forget about showering and cleaning and cooking when she retreated into her current project. Knowing that made her feel guilty, which had resulted in fewer books written throughout the course of her marriage.

She hadn't written anything of merit since Eric's death, didn't even have any ideas. The work she'd done in South Carolina wasn't anything she was proud of, so she wouldn't let anyone see it unless she found some motivation to make it something worthwhile. Her editors were pushing her for a new manuscript, her readers were emailing and sending Facebook messages begging for the next book in this series or that, but creativity wasn't something she'd been capable of lately. And now, even though she'd retreated into her writer habits, she'd done so without actually working.

Feeling somewhat revived after the shower, Izz dressed in a pair of jeans and black tank top, sighing when her phone buzzed. Olivia and Deanna had been bugging her lately about going out to dinner as a group, as though they hadn't all just spent a week together in Myrtle Beach. She suspected they wanted to make sure she hadn't slipped back into depressed mode since returning home. Avoiding them meant she wouldn't have to deal with the scrutiny of having done just that.

Glancing at the phone, she saw the same blocked number and grit her teeth together as she read the message that stated, *Smart choice returning home. But we are not done yet.*

"Oh, really," she muttered, fingers gripping the phone tightly enough that they began to ache. "How about we put an end to it right fucking now."

Barely taking the time to brush her hair and put on shoes, Izz drove on autopilot to her late husband's former office, knowing the route by heart. After slamming into a parking space and stomping in the front door, Izz headed straight for the stairs, too impatient to wait for the elevator to the third floor. She ascended quickly, shoving open the door to the main lobby, her anger never dissipating, not when she stalked past the secretary without replying to her frantic protest, not when she threw open the office door for one Breckan Bex.

She hadn't been back to the office since Eric's death, not even to retrieve his belongings. Bex had taken care of packing up the room and bringing the boxes to Izz, the one halfway decent thing he'd done since she'd known him.

"Enough games, Bex," she growled, standing in front of the desk and glaring down at the man she'd come to hate over the past decade.

Bex, whose eyes had widened in surprise when she stormed in then narrowed in amusement, quickly ended the call he was on and stood. "Well, Miss Isabella. To what do I owe the pleasure?"

"Cut the shit," she replied, not at all phased by his smooth, charmingly accented question. "I don't know how you pulled it off, but your messages are going to stop. And you sure as hell aren't going to follow me around anymore."

The amusement in his expression morphed into annoyance. "What are you talking about?"

Hands on her hips, Izz hardened her own face into a warning of what was to come. "I'm done with your childish messages and I sure as hell won't tolerate another little shadow dance on the beach. Keep your distance, or I swear on Eric's grave I will fucking end you."

He slowly rounded the desk, stepping closer to Izz until he was staring down at her. "I don't take kindly to threats, lass."

"Consider it a promise," she growled back. "Stay the fuck away from me, Breckan Bex. This is your last warning."

Bex looked up as though considering her words.

"Perhaps you have something I want."

"Perhaps you want my foot up your ass." When he only smiled down at her, Izz let out a disgusted sigh. "You know, I thought that after Eric died you'd leave me the hell alone. As if losing him wasn't hard enough that I wanted to die right along with him, you have to come along and be a fucking jerk on top of it. Way to rub salt in the wound, asshole."

His expression almost softened before turning bitter. "I think it's time you leave, Izz."

"Don't have to tell me twice." She spun on her heel and stalked to the door, stopping when his voice sounded behind her.

"You're not the only one who lost him, you know."

A dozen snarky replies floated across her mind, but she couldn't speak any of them. Instead, Izz merely turned her head slightly and whispered, "It sure as hell feels that way," before slipping out the door.

THE NEXT DAY, AFTER SEVERAL texts from Olivia threatening to come drag her out by her hair, Izz agreed to dinner at a local café. All five were there before she arrived, which she found suspicious, since she was at least ten minutes early.

Plastering on a smile, Izz took a seat at the center of the table and greeted her friends, giving a quick drink order to the waiter. "Alright, let's get this over with," she said to the collective. "I'm showered, I've eaten at least two meals a day, I haven't had a single nightmare, and I even called my evil grandmother the other day. Satisfied?"

They all glanced around at one another and nodded. It

was as simple as that, and their conversation changed to the usual.

"We enrolled in a self-defense class," Beth informed Izz, pointing at her sister. "Gonna kick some bad guy ass, though I hope we never have to."

"I found me a hot young thing who wants nothing more than a piece of ass every now and then," Miley put in, flipping her hair with a saucy pout.

"I'm considering a tattoo," Olivia added, though Izz already knew – and was shocked by – that.

All eyes turned to Deanna, who was pushing around a fry on her plate. "No updates?" Izz asked.

"Oh she has one alright," Miley cut in with a grin, smirking at the glare Deanna shot her way. "It seems little Miss D got the D in Myrtle Beach and never even told us."

Izz's eyes widened as the others started laughing, Deanna hiding her face behind her hand. "Who was it? Josh? When? At the beach?"

"Yes and yes," Miley answered for a silent Deanna. "They're in *loooove*."

"Oh, shut up," Deanna finally spoke up. "It's not love. It was just having fun."

While she could have called her friend a hypocrite, Izz decided to just go with it. "Those knights know their way around a bedroom, huh?"

"Or a shoreline." Deanna snorted at her own words and the others joined in, all previous tensions forgotten.

SURPRISINGLY, SHE RETURNED HOME IN high spirits, pleased to have eased her friends' worries and happy with the flow of conversation. She loved her girls, even if they could be pushy in their checkups.

Locking the door behind her, Izz did her usual sweep of the house. She'd always been suspicious, never able to sleep until she made sure nothing was out of order. Since she rarely used any room other than the bedroom, kitchen, master bathroom, and living room, her sweeps didn't typically take long.

This time, though, she stopped in the living room in front of her father's sword. It looked so skimpy there compared to Cade's massive collection, but held the same pride for her nonetheless. Reaching out, Izz traced a finger down the cool blade, remembering the day her father entrusted her with its care.

"The legacy has always been yours, Isabella," he'd told her. *"I've trained you in history. I've trained you in swordplay and self-defense, as were the ways of our ancestors. I've trained you in caring for the memories entrusted to us. But I cannot train you to open your heart and trust the love it feels. That, you must do on your own."*

She hadn't understood what he meant then, simply nodding as he spoke and told her of their legacy as he imagined it, as he'd done so many times before. He believed deeply that their family came from the days of the dragons, as he called them, back when old women created prophecies, and swords with long-lost names were passed down throughout the generations. She hadn't told Cade that, was afraid to admit what it meant that their families were so connected to a similar past.

"Our family was there, back in the days when dragons roamed," her father would tell her as he stood at the stove or sat hunched over a drawing. *"Our ancestors lived the love between knights and their maidens. To them, sto-*

ries about love reincarnated in souls thousands of years down the line weren't stories. They were a way of life. Can you imagine, Isabella? Can you imagine a love so strong, it is destined to survive thousands of years?"

She couldn't, not then and not now. Love was fleeting. Love was destructive. Love was rooting in the heart she didn't trust.

"Son of a bitch," she whispered.

Chapter 21.

IT WAS DARK BY THE time Izz pulled up at Cade's beach house in her rental car, opting to park on the street and walk up the long drive. Having booked the first flight to Myrtle Beach the previous night, she managed to arrive back in South Carolina close to dinnertime the next day, the entire time refusing to let her thoughts talk her into turning around and hiding beneath the covers in the safety of her own home. She was exhausted from travel and hungry, but had refused to stop until she reached her destination.

All but the light over the door was off when she walked up the steps of the front porch, but she knocked anyway. When silence met her ears, she glanced at her phone to check the time, remembering that he likely had a show for at least another half hour, and wouldn't be home for another hour after that. With a resigned sigh, Izz sat down on the porch swing to wait, knowing if she went back to her car and drove around to pass the time, she might not return.

After just over an hour passed, Izz had moved from the porch swing to the bench to the wicker chair, anxious and nervous. She rested her elbows on her knees and leaned forward, leg shaking as she waited. Mind racing with what she would say, ultimately deciding that it all sounded idiotic. Maybe she would just stand there and stare and wait for him to say something. Or just run away. Right now that sounded like the most viable option considering the way her stomach was clenching and her hands were shaking.

When headlights finally pierced the darkness, she sucked in a deep breath and leapt to her feet, her gut churning in almost painful anticipation. She still had no idea what she'd say or do. All her waiting hadn't afforded her anything clever.

Despite her nerves, a smile crept across her face when she saw Cade step out of the car, dressed in jeans and a loose shirt, looking like all he wanted was a shower and a bed. That smile faded when a second person emerged from the passenger side, a dark-haired beauty who was laughing at something he must have said before exiting the vehicle.

"Yeah, yeah," he was replying good-naturedly, just as Izz was trying to figure out how the hell to get away unseen. "Just you wait until–"

His words cut off when he glanced up, his dark eyes latching onto Izz standing on his front porch. For a few seconds they merely stared, one with an expression of surprise, one with hurt and humiliation in her eyes.

"Isabella," he whispered, not sure if that single word was a statement or a question.

"I ... I'm sorry," Izz said quickly, embarrassment burning her cheeks. "I thought ... I should go." She'd expected him to be upset, maybe even turn her away, but she'd never even considered he might have moved on so quickly.

"Isabella," Cade said again, taking a step forward to stop her when she made to hurry down the steps, but unable to find his voice when he saw the tears in her eyes. He didn't know what had caused them, or what to say to make them disappear.

"So *this* is the famous Isabella," the dark-haired beauty said from behind him, saving them both from having to speak in that moment. "No wonder Cade won't shut up about you. You are positively gorgeous."

Confused, Izz moved her gaze to the other woman, brow furrowing. "…What?"

The woman laughed and joined her on the porch, holding out a hand. "My name is Brynn, owner of the ugliest shirt you've ever seen."

The pit in the bottom of her stomach started to fade as Izz pieced the words together in her exhausted mind. "You're … Cade's sister?"

"The one and only," Brynn affirmed with a wink, then held her arms out at her sides. "With much better fashion these days, don't you think?"

Relief flooded her as Izz scanned the outfit, a snazzy red dress that hugged her curves. "Uh, yeah, it's beautiful. About the shirt—"

"Don't even worry about it." Brynn waved her off with a hand. "But as I can see my oh-so-charming brother here is completely at a loss for words, I'm going to take that as my cue to head on out. Call me tomorrow, Cade." With that, she strolled to her car, which Izz hadn't even seen tucked away off to the far right of the driveway, and sped off into the night.

Alone now, Cade seemed to find his voice. "What are

you doing here?"

Though she'd been hoping to hear happiness in his voice, she was glad there was no anger or resentment, only confusion. Unsure how to respond, Izz managed a shrug, wishing he would come up the steps instead of stare at her from the front walk. "You asked me to stay."

"You left."

Now there was resentment in the reply, she noted as she took in a deep breath and pressed her lips together. "I came back," she said quietly.

Cade stared up at her through slightly narrowed eyes, as though considering her words. "Why?"

Izz huffed and crossed her arms, now slightly irritated – and annoyed that she was annoyed. "Because when I got home I realized that I made a mistake and that I needed to stop being so damn afraid, okay?" she snapped. "Maybe I just needed a few days to make the decision mine. But I'm here now … if you still want me."

Before she could comprehend his actions, Cade had sprung up the steps and wrapped his arms around her, pressing his lips to hers in a deep, rough kiss. There was desperation in his actions, desperation mixed with need and urgency that she met just as passionately.

"Isabella," Cade whispered against her lips, "I will always want you." Taking her by the hand, he led her inside, locking the door behind them. "As much as I want to continue this, and talk about what brought you back, I desperately need a shower. The show was a bit rough tonight and Brynn was rushing me out the door. Seems she has a date tonight."

Izz smiled when he lifted a hand to cup the side of her face, any worry she'd had about his reaction to her arrival melting away. "To be continued, then."

He left her in the kitchen without another word. She sat at the counter for a few minutes, listening to the sound of the water upstairs. The rush of seeing and kissing him had been replaced by a strange sense of being brushed off, and she wondered if he really did just want a shower or if he needed time to figure out what to do with her.

"Well, then," she muttered, sliding off the stool. Izz climbed the stairs quickly, following the echoes of running water until she stood just outside the bathroom. In two swift movements her clothes were off and she was gently pushing open the door, heart pounding as she silently prayed Cade wouldn't reject what she was about to do. She could see his shadow on the other side of the curtain, oblivious to her presence until she lifted the curtain and stepped inside.

"What are you ... doing," Cade asked, his voice trailing off as he turned and caught sight of her naked body standing before him.

"I'm staying."

Izz stepped closer, lifting her hands to his shoulders and herself to her toes as she kissed him softly. She felt his grip on her hips, hesitant at first, then tightening. Taking command, she sought entry to his mouth and was rewarded as she reveled in the familiar taste of him.

"Isabella," Cade whispered, breaking the kiss and resting his forehead on hers. Warm water cascaded down his neck and shoulders, his dark and wet hair clinging to skin. "We need to talk about this. About what you coming back means."

"It means I want to be with you. What else matters?"

When he didn't answer, Izz shot him an almost sinful

grin and kissed him again, moving her lips from his mouth to his chin, his throat, the broad lines of his shoulder, careful to avoid the bruises that marred his flesh from his time in the arena. At the same time her hands moved south, tracing the muscles in his chest and stomach, trailing across hip bones until he shivered even in the hot spray of water, then finding all of him hard and ready for her touch.

Izz looked up at him, seeing the lust in his eyes warring with the questions, the struggle to stop and talk or let her do exactly what her hands were promising as she slowly, tantalizingly, began to massage his cock. His jaw clenched when her grip tightened ever so slightly, a gruff sound escaping his throat and his hands clenching on her waist. Grinning again, Izz lowered herself to her knees.

"Isabella," Cade said, her name leaving his tongue as a sound of both hesitation and want.

"Tell me to stop," she replied, and when he merely closed his eyes in response, she took him in her mouth, one hand cupping him, the other mimicking the stroking of her mouth. She enjoyed this new taste of him, the feel of each throb against her lips, the way his fingers fisted in her hair and directed her movements. Faster, slower, deeper, agonizingly slow, until she understood what he wanted and made each move her own.

When she heard a thud above her, Izz looked up through long, wet lashes. Cade had slammed a fist against the shower wall, his head braced on his arm, dark eyes roving her body – tracing the water as it trailed down the sides of her face, over the swell of her breasts, down her stomach to the spread of her legs – until returning to her face, watching her closely. Their gaze met briefly and the corners of her mouth upturned. The grin urged them both on, Cade moving his hips in tune with her, Izz releasing a hum of approval that reverberated through him, eliciting a groan as she sucked him harder.

Pulling back only slightly, Izz ran her tongue around the sensitive tip until she knew he couldn't stand the teasing any longer. Then she worked him harder, waiting for the moment he would tighten his hold and give her the sign. When he did, she only took him deeper and matched his moans until she felt him spilling inside her, warmth filling her mouth.

Cade, fully sated, took a moment to slump against the wall while Izz lifted herself to her feet, turning them both so she stood in the water, letting it soak her hair, her body. Wordlessly she handed him the bar of soap from the shelf and he took his cue, lathering it on his hands before sliding them across her body. He paid special care to her breasts, massaging both at once, taking each nipple between his teeth one at a time. Finally his fingers found her center and he stroked her as she had stroked him.

"Your turn, m'lady," he rasped in her ear in that deep, throaty voice she had come to love.

"No," she answered, putting a hand to his chest. "That was just for you. Now, we talk."

Chapter 22

HE ORDERED A PIZZA WHILE Izz finished showering, shampooing and conditioning her long hair to get the feel of airport traveling off her body. As she toweled off and redressed in the same clothes, she found herself lingering in the bathroom, nervous of what this "talk" would bring.

By the time she made her way back to the kitchen, Cade was setting out plates and napkins, his jaw clenched and his brow furrowed. She watched him for a moment, the way he moved from cabinet to cabinet and drawer to drawer, the way he seemed so flustered yet tried so hard to appear nonchalant.

"Cade," she said softly, not wanting to frazzle him more than he already was. His nerves made hers worse. "Cade," she tried again, and again was unsuccessful. Finally she put her hand on his arm, stopping him from whatever the hell he was doing with the silverware. She waited until he looked up to ask, "Are you going to ask me to leave?"

Her question seemed to snap him out of his trance. In response, his arm snaked around her waist and he yanked her against him, crushing his mouth to hers. She opened to him, melding her body to his, letting him take whatever he wanted from her.

"You aren't going anywhere," he all but growled, face buried in her hair. "I'm not letting you get away so easily this time, m'lady."

Izz laughed lightly. "Then why do you seem so upset? I mean, you have every right to be mad at me, but I'm not sure what all *this* is about." She gestured to the forks and spoons he'd put out – for eating pizza.

Cade followed her gaze, then shook his head at himself. "I asked you to stay … but I never considered what would happen if you did." At her questioning stare, he continued. "To be honest, I've never done this before, asking a woman to stay and all. I want to be everything you need, Isabella."

Charmed, though a bit miffed, Izz wrapped her arms around his neck and stared up at him. "I just need you to be with me," she replied honestly. "I don't need you to save me or be something more than you are. I just need you. We'll figure the rest out eventually."

They spent the rest of the night in each other's arms. Eating pizza, sharing stories of their pasts and laughing as they made up their own fairy tales, exploring every part of their bodies together. Though Izz had reserved a hotel room just in case, Cade insisted she stay with him. Demanded, she considered wryly as she watched him sleep, until it almost felt creepy to do so any longer. Instead she curled up next to him, breathed in the scent of saltwater and sexy man, and fell asleep feeling like she was finally home.

THE SUN HAD BARELY BROKEN over the horizon when Izz stirred the next morning, surprised to see Cade brushing his teeth in the bathroom. Never much of a morning person, she merely closed her eyes and waited for him to emerge before pushing herself to her elbows.

"Why are you up so damn early?" she asked, her voice rough with sleep. "There isn't even any sun." Vaguely she wondered how awful she looked, but decided she didn't care. He asked her to stay, he could deal with her early-morning disheveled look.

Cade smiled and sat next to her on the edge of the bed. "I have to go to work. We are starting a week-long training camp for our new hires. It runs until five, then I'm all yours. I don't participate in the show while I'm running the camp, so I won't be performing this week."

Izz rolled over onto her back and looked up at him. His face was shadowed in the dark bedroom, making the angles of his face even more mysterious. "Sounds not fun at all," she said around a yawn.

"In the meantime," he continued with a laugh, "you are going to go check out of that hotel, bring the rest of your luggage back here, and make yourself comfortable."

"Yes, sir," she replied mockingly, though she was looking forward to the idea of doing just that. "I need to work anyway. Haven't been inspired to write lately, but I'm think today I will be."

One corner of his mouth lifting, Cade traced a hand up her stomach until his fingers circled her breasts. "Inspiration, m'lady?"

She heard the invitation in his words. "You have a camp to run."

With a sound of disappointment, Cade withdrew his

hand, opting instead for a chaste kiss on her forehead. "Tonight, then, you're all mine."

Chapter 23

TEN HOURS LATER CADE RETURNED home, exhausted but excited. For the first time, he wasn't coming home alone to an empty house with merely a promise of what could be. No, for the first time, there was someone waiting for him, and he couldn't wait to see that someone again.

Muffled voices met his ears when he opened the door, and he followed the sound to one of the spare rooms that served as a makeshift office that he rarely used. Pushing the door open, Cade bit back a chuckle when he saw Izz perched on the edge of the recliner, her legs twisted in a way that looked horribly uncomfortable to him but seemed to work for her, a laptop resting on the ottoman in front of her. A flower-patterned blanket – another of his sister's rejects – was wrapped around her shoulders, her hair piled in a messy bun atop her head, her fingers working furiously over the keyboard. She looked adorable, he thought, her face scrunched in concentration, her body rocking slightly as though in tune with her inner thoughts. How she could think with the sounds of revving cars blaring on the TV was beyond him.

When he saw the mess around her, he could only shake his head. Izz had told him about her tendency to get lost in writer mode, and he could see now she wasn't joking. A few cans of Coke sat on the floor next to the table, along with empty wrappers and a half-eaten sub on the table. He figured she must have gone shopping at some point, because all that junk food certainly didn't belong to him.

Quietly, Cade eased himself out of the room, shutting the door behind him. Though he wanted nothing more than to go to her and take her in his arms, he also wanted this to be her home too, and that meant giving them both the time and space to create their own routines.

Izz wasn't sure what time it was when she surfaced, but guessed it was late. Normally she would've kept writing, having finally found her flow again, but she worried what Cade would think. She emerged from her makeshift office and found Cade in the living room, sitting on the couch with a beer in one hand, the other propped up along the back of the couch. He glanced over his shoulder when she entered, watching her as she rounded the corner and lowered herself to the cushions, laying down and resting her head on his thigh.

"Guess I lost track of time," she said, staring at the TV. It looked like a history program, which she would likely find completely dull.

"I see you commandeered my office," he laughed back. "You were in the zone. I didn't want to disturb you."

"Sorry," she said again. "It's just where I ended up."

"No need to apologize," he said lightly, taking a swig of beer. "It's your house too."

They sat in comfortable silence for a few minutes, his

fingers playing with her hair as they watched television. The blonde locks drifted across her shoulders, spilling over his leg, brushing against her cheek as she shifted her position to get more comfortable. Gently, he reached over and tucked that errant strand behind her ear, watching as she smiled. He settled back and turned his attention back to the documentary.

"Cade?"

"Yes, m'lady?"

"This is the most boring show in the history of boring shows."

His laughter filled the room, echoing through her in tendrils of deep pleasure. He handed her the remote and settled back, and in that moment she knew she wanted to keep this man hers forever.

HUMMING QUIETLY TO HERSELF, OLIVIA jogged up the steps to her best friend's house and knocked, impatiently hopping from foot to foot while she waited. Behind her, Miley matched her tune, both of them starting to sing off tune while they waited.

After a couple minutes Olivia frowned and knocked again, then rolled her eyes. "If that woman is in bed, I swear to God," she muttered under her breath, pulling out her spare key and letting them both into Izz's house. It was commonplace for Olivia to enter her friend's freely and vice-versa, though there was always the chance of catching the other stepping out of the shower stark naked, which had happened on more than one occasion.

Olivia stepped inside, immediately feeling the emptiness. Usually a television was on somewhere in the house;

Izz couldn't stand silence. "Izz?"

"Izzy girl!" Miley shouted loud enough to be heard in any nook or cranny of the house. She shrugged when there was no reply. "We're either being ignored or she's not here."

Together they walked the halls, checking the main rooms their friend was usually in before Olivia finally pulled her phone from her pocket.

Are you dead?

While she waited for Izz to reply to her text, Olivia found herself making the rounds just like her friend always did. For a while after Eric's death, Olivia had been the one to take care of Izz, looking after woman and home when the grieving widow was unable to get out of bed. In the past Izz had always been the one to take charge and do whatever needed doing. Olivia had been happy to finally let Izz be the one being looked after, though she'd wished it could have been under different circumstances.

Her phone chirped from her hand and she glanced at the screen and the message that read, *Out of town.*

Out of town, off on a day drive, or out of town, can't get enough knight sword?

None of your business, you dirty degenerate.

Olivia's eyes widened and she showed the text to Miley, both of them laughing to themselves, the sound echoing off the walls. Pure elation coursed through them at the thought of her friend finally taking a chance. Maybe it wasn't love, maybe it was just lust after a year of not getting laid, but it was better than nothing.

"Well, you aren't who I expected to find."

The laughter abruptly cut off at the sound of a man's voice behind her. Olivia spun around, half surprised, half not when she saw Bex standing in the entryway. At her side, Miley crossed her arms and gave the man her best 'I want to kill you' glare.

"What the hell are you doing in here?" Olivia sneered.

"The door was open. I was worried."

She knew it was a flat-out lie. The door was never open. Izz had reamed her out more than once for leaving the door ajar, and Olivia never made that mistake anymore. Though it was entirely possible that she left it unlocked. "Bullshit. Get the fuck out before I call the cops. I should call them anyway, with you breaking and entering."

"Don't be so dramatic." Bex waved her off with a hand, brushing back a few locks of perfectly golden hair. "I'm only here to find Izz."

"Why?"

"Because she seems to be under the impression that threatening me in my office is acceptable behavior."

Miley scoffed at that, tossing her wild curls over her shoulder. "Well, stop being such a douche and she wouldn't have to." She moved closer until they were mere inches apart and her pointer finger was poking him in the chest. "I don't appreciate you trying to screw everything up for her. Izz is one of my best friends and I swear to God if you hurt her or even serve as a minor annoyance in her day that I will make your life a living hell."

Bex eyed the redhead closely, admiring her tough stance, the way she glared at him like a momma bird protecting her young. He'd met her before at some party or another, but never really paid her much attention given that she was Izz's friend. Now he was wondering why he'd been so willing to skip this one over.

"Maybe we forget this whole thing, and go out to lunch instead."

For a moment Miley merely stared at him, both disgusted and amused, while Olivia rolled her eyes and sighed. "Are you seriously asking me out? After you stalk and harass my friend and all but break into her house?" She removed her finger from his chest and stepped back. "You want me to forget this whole thing? Leave Izz alone."

"But then we won't get to have these charming conversations."

Tired of his stalling, and suspicious of the way Bex was looking at Miley with that piercing stare of his, Olivia stepped in front of her friend. "Tell you what, Bex. You get the fuck out, and maybe I don't call the cops. But next time, you can bet your ass you will be behind bars within the hour."

"As you wish, lass," Bex conceded with a bow of his head, his eyes never leaving Miley. "Perhaps you'd like to show me out? Make sure I leave quietly, and all."

The request was said to Miley, who nodded to Olivia. The other woman was far too riled up to respond, so she retreated to the kitchen. Miley all but shoved the man out the front door but couldn't help one last comment. "You know, you're a decent-looking guy with a good job and decent brains, Bex. If you weren't such a piece of shit, women might actually give a damn about you."

Claiming the final word, Miley slammed the door in his face.

Chapter 24

THE SCENT OF ITALIAN FOOD broke Izz from her writing reverie. She slid off her headphones and stretched, glancing at the clock, not at all surprised to see that five hours had passed since she sat down with her laptop. She'd long since claimed the den as her writing cave and Cade didn't appear to mind, as it seemed he only used the room to store random pieces of furniture.

After making sure her latest manuscript – a daring tale about a knight fighting to save his true love – was saved, Izz followed her nose into the kitchen.

"You cook?" It wasn't the most graceful of greetings, but she hadn't seen Cade cook in the short time she'd known him.

Cade turned to face her, spatula in hand. "Lasagna, m'lady. It's the only halfway fancy thing I can cook," he added wryly.

Izz sidled up next to him, breathing in the fresh-out-of-the-oven meal. "Smells delicious."

Cade shooed her away, gesturing toward the table while he served up two plates of lasagna and garlic bread. Following his orders, Izz took a seat and watched him work, thoroughly impressed. They ate in amicable silence for a few minutes until Izz broached the subject she'd been thinking about all day.

"So," she began, pushing around a bite of pasta with her fork, "I was thinking … When is your slow season?"

With a curious smile, Cade swallowed and lifted a shoulder. "I'm the boss. If I want it to be my slow season, then it is. Why do you ask?"

Izz shrugged. "I was just thinking, we should go on a trip sometime."

"What kind of trip?"

"Ocoee River in Tennessee, white-water rafting."

Cade took a sip of the red wine he'd poured just before sitting down. "That's … specific." When her face fell, he quickly added, "I would love to go. I was just surprised you knew where already."

Izz took in a deep breath, blowing it out quietly. "My parents used to take me every year. It was our thing, you know? I haven't been back to that particular river since they died. I thought maybe you would enjoy it. It's beautiful out there, surrounded by nature and wildlife, rafting down the river. Total adrenaline rush, but also quiet too in spots if you–"

"Isabella," he cut in softly. "You don't have to justify it. Of course I'll go." Elated but trying to hide her excitement, Izz turned back to her food. Cade wanted to keep her talking. He couldn't get enough of the sound of her voice, the way her tone held such conviction and life. "So what did you do today? Lots of writing?"

"Writing, junk food eating." She grinned when Cade shook his head, amused. The only snacks he kept around were fruits and vegetables, and he'd certainly noticed the salty and sugary additions to the pantry. "I ordered a couple things for my bedroom. I'll have Olivia send me a few things soon, but I … What?" she asked when she saw the grimace cross his face.

Setting down his fork and trying to maintain a calm exterior, Cade looked across the table at the woman staring at him like he was crazy. "Your bedroom?" he repeated. "I thought we discussed this."

Instantly contrite, Izz fell back against the chair and stared at her hands. "We did," she answered, thinking back to the argument they'd had her second day there when she asked for her own room, rather than moving into his. "I thought we had it settled."

"You have it settled," he corrected her. "I'm still waiting."

"For what?"

"For you to truly be here with me."

At that, Izz looked up, aggravation spread across her face. "What is that supposed to mean? I'm right here."

"Are you?" No longer hungry, Cade pushed his plate away. "You show up on my doorstep wanting to be with me. You want to plan trips with me. You want to sleep with me, but you don't want to *sleep* with me."

"Cade," Izz said on a sigh, bracing her head in her hands. It was a foolish argument, considering she shared his bed most nights anyway, but knowing she had her own room made it feel less real, a safety net of sorts. But she didn't know how to explain that to him so she avoided it altogether. "Cade … Are we crazy for doing this? I mean, you hardly know this woman who shows up on your doorstep, yet you take her in as though you've known her your entire life. I drop everything for a man I've known a week and expect him to naturally accept all the fucked-up baggage I come with. What were we thinking?"

Feeling that she was avoiding a real answer rather than actually posing the question, Cade sat back and crossed his arms, staring at her inquisitively. "I was thinking this beautiful, arrogant, fascinating, space cadet of a woman waltzed into my life and turned it completely upside down. I was thinking she was the one I'd been waiting for, the one I've known my whole life, even if I only just met her."

Frustrated, both because she didn't want to discuss this and because she knew he was right, Izz pushed out of the chair. "I don't want to talk about this anymore."

He mimicked her reaction. "Then what do you want, Isabella?"

Staring at him, Izz realized she didn't have an answer. She wanted … him, not him; freedom, a partner; independence, someone to come home to; to make memories with someone new, to never let go of the one she loved first.

The conflict played across her face, a portrait of unmasked emotion. Cade saw every one and, though he couldn't read her mind, knew she wasn't going to answer him. "When you figure it out, you know where to find me," he said, then left her at the table.

FEELING GUILTY AS WELL AS mad, Izz cleaned up their half-eaten dinner then went to bed, alone. She'd moved her things in to the room three down from Cade's when she first arrived, still not completely sure why. At the time, it seemed like the only logical choice. After all, they barely knew each other and needed to take things slow … even if they were living together. Cade hadn't been pleased with the arrangement, and said so more than once, but she wasn't budging.

Despite her feelings of righteousness, Izz slept fitfully, wrapped up in a blanket that wasn't hers, dreaming of things she could never have again. When she awoke, the house was empty, Cade having left for work already.

Izz bypassed her own work for the day, opting for a long walk on the beach instead. A few people were out with their dogs, and she laughed as the canines bounded into the waves, chasing Frisbees or nothing at all. Being a weekend, there were plenty of parents with their children. She'd crossed the idea of kids off her wish list a long time ago after being told she couldn't have them anyway, but she could appreciate the love shown from a mother and father.

The truth was, she missed family. The way her parents made her feel safe, happy, wanted. The way they looked at each other, as though nothing else could possibly exist in the world except each other. Even as a child, a wild child with a tendency to act without thinking, Izz wanted that.

Once upon a time she thought she found it with Eric, though even on her wedding day she'd known that the spark her father always talked about, *the spark that makes your heart hurt just being away from them*, he'd always said, wasn't there. She'd been so lonely after her parents died, and Eric had been there to make her feel special, not alone anymore.

She'd come to love him too, and appreciate him, admire and respect his gentleness and intelligence, his steadfast conviction of good in the world. In time she became excited to hear his key in the door, the feel of his kiss against her cheek, the sound of his teasing when she spent the entire day writing…

"But it's all over now," Izz whispered. She'd made her way to the shoreline, her toes barely touching wet sand. "I'm tired of feeling guilty for feelings that I can't control. I'm tired of holding back because it seems like the right thing to do. I'm tired of not living, all to preserve a memory of what once was."

With a sigh, Izz took a step forward so that the water sloshed over her ankles. "I'll always love you, Eric. But I have to love me too." She closed her eyes and pictured her late husband. His smile, the blue of his eyes, that lanky frame always too awkward for its own good. And, with his picture smiling back at her, Izz whispered her final good-bye.

Chapter

25

SHE MADE HER WAY TO *Quest* by lunchtime, eager to see and speak with Cade. Maybe she'd even get to watch some of their practices.

Cynthia let her in with a wink and a grin, leading her to one of the back rooms. "Mr. Cadian!" she called to a group of men standing in a circle around a sparring pit.

At the entrance to the pit, Cade turned, seeing the two women waiting for him. He said something to one of the other men before heading over. Cynthia excused herself as he approached. "What's up?"

Izz smiled, wanting to go in for a kiss but unsure how it would go over in front of his employees. So she simply stood there, hands tucked into her back pockets. "I thought maybe we could grab some lunch and talk about a couple things. I wanted to tell you something."

Cade glanced over his shoulder. "Can it wait until to-night? We have another hour of practice before we break, and I need to be here to go over the routines."

Disappointed, Izz nodded. "Sure. I'll see you at home?"

"Right." That was all he offered before he walked

back to the guys.

Though she understood why he was being short with her, it didn't take away the sting. Izz sighed and turned. She stopped when she saw the knight standing behind her holding a bottle of water. "Hey, Rowan."

"Izz," he greeted, taking a sip. "Come to see Cade?"

"Just saying hi." She didn't want to admit the truth, that he wasn't interested in saying hi back.

Rowan stared at her for a moment. "It's a stressful week, getting all the new guys trained."

"I suppose."

As though sensing the hurt in her voice, Rowan continued. "I've known Cade for a while. I've never seen him this happy. I know it's corny, but he's a better guy with you, a lot happier. Just ...don't take him for granted. Don't fuck with him, you know?"

Touched, Izz looked up at the young man offering words of advice wiser than his years. He looked so boyish and, yet, so somber. "Thanks, Rowan. That means a lot." She nudged him with her shoulder, then, sending one last look at Cade's back, headed for home.

THREE HOURS LATER THE FRONT door opened and slammed shut. Izz jumped up from the chair in the den, smoothing back her hair, strangely nervous. She bounded down the stairs, swinging around the corner and into the kitchen, where Cade was pulling a bottle of water out of the fridge.

"Hey," she greeted, almost out of breath, though she wasn't sure if it was from excitement or rushing downstairs. When he merely nodded in her direction, she continued. "So, I wanted to show you something." The coy smile on her face fell when he grabbed his keys.

"I have to meet Brynn for dinner. I just stopped by the house because I forgot my wallet."

Izz drummed her fingers on the counter. The brush-off was obvious, and it infuriated her, though she tried to push down the anger since she understood where his hesitance was coming from. "It will only take a second. I think you'll like it."

"Later, Isabella."

With that, he turned and walked back out, not seeing the way her expression changed to one of hurt, or perhaps not letting himself see it.

Cade made the drive to his favorite Mediterranean restaurant, meeting his sister inside at their usual table. She was waiting for him, and smiled when he leaned over to kiss her cheek.

"I ordered for us, the usual."

"Sounds good."

"No Isabella?" she asked, pouting a bit. "I thought you said she was back in town."

"She is. She's at home."

Brynn wasn't willing to let him go so easily. "Why didn't she come?"

Cade sighed. "We had a bit of a … disagreement." Briefly, he explained their fight, only because he knew Brynn would press him for details until he gave in anyway.

While she listened, Brynn toyed with her fork, staring at her brother with a look of exasperation. "So, what did she want to tell you before you blew out of the house?"

"Don't know."

"Aren't you curious?" He was, but didn't want to admit it. "Roarke Cadian, are you serious. Why didn't you take two seconds to hear her out? Whatever she had to say, it could have been just what you've been waiting to hear."

Cade shrugged, pausing to let the waiter place their plates down in front of them. "I don't know what to expect, Brynn. I keep thinking, maybe I made it too easy on her, you know?"

"What do you mean?"

"I mean, I made it pretty clear from the beginning that I wanted her. I opened up my home to her, basically gave her an open invitation into my life. And she fucking shredded it to pieces."

Brynn regarded him with a smirk. "Big brother, stop being so dramatic. Not every woman is going to fall madly in love with you with just one look and be all weak in the knees because a handsome knight called her *m'lady*. You think you made it too easy on her, I think she's making you work for it, and you don't want to. You want it to be easy instead of having to work for it."

"I'll work as hard as I have to."

"Oh really?" Brynn looked across the table at her brother, one perfectly sculpted brow lifted. "So ... what the hell are you still doing here?"

THE HOUSE WAS DARK WHEN Cade returned home, having excused himself from his bi-monthly dinner early with a promise to bring Izz to the next one, assuming she'd even want to after the way he'd brushed her aside earlier. He entered quietly, listening for any indication of her presence, hearing only the ocean.

Making his way to the back of the house, he saw the

sliding door open to the deck. He followed the sound of waves crashing and stepped outside, finding Izz stretched out on one of the lounge chairs, apparently asleep. When he saw the wine bottle next to her, he knew why. She wasn't one to drink much, so he guessed she was going to have one hell of a hangover in the morning.

Shaking his head as much at himself as at her, Cade kneeled down and touched her shoulder. "M'lady," he whispered against her ear. "Tis not safe for a beautiful damsel to be asleep outside and alone."

Izz stirred slightly, turning her face into the hand cupping her cheek. "You're home?"

Cade answered the kind-of question with one of his own. "You're drunk?"

A rare giggle escaped Izz as she turned, eyes opening briefly before closing again. "Just a little. But you love me anyway."

Her words froze him, and he wasn't sure she even realized what she said. "Maybe I do," he whispered, sliding one arm under her legs and the other behind her back, lifting her easily from the chair. "Come on, let's get you to bed."

Cade navigated the house carefully, Izz's head tucked against his shoulder in a gesture that felt so familiar and comfortable that he nearly couldn't stand it. At the top of the stairs he readjusted her in his arms and she motioned to move. "Stay put," he ordered. "I'll bring you to your room."

"No," Izz mumbled as she snuggled closer to him. "To our room."

Frowning, Cade carried her to his room and stepped inside, using his elbow to flick on the light. As the room filled with a dim glow, he glanced around to see the subtle but reaffirming changes. The dresser was topped with little knickknacks that weren't his own. A small bookshelf had been added to the far corner. Two blankets were draped over a chair overlooking the beach. A picture of a couple with their little girl sat on the nightstand on the right side of the bed. A stuffed penguin rested on the pillow.

This was what she'd wanted to show him earlier, he realized as guilt washed over him. She'd taken the next step and moved into his room, and he'd blown her off.

Sighing lightly, Cade laid Izz down on the side of the bed she'd clearly chosen as her own, tucking the blanket around her and handing her the stuffed animal. He smiled as she curled her arms around it, already fast asleep.

Chapter 26

THE SOUND OF PANS AND plates clanging together
woke Izz the next morning. She got up slowly, a headache
already brewing behind her eyes. As she trudged to the
bathroom, she was surprised that the headache was the
worst of it, that she wasn't struggling to keep down last
night's dinner as well.

With unhurried movements, Izz brushed her teeth and
used the bathroom, not bothering to change out of her
sweats and threadbare tank top that had certainly seen better days, or even brush her hair. A loose braid would suffice for whatever came next.

It was only when she exited the bathroom that she realized where she was. Glancing around, Izz took in a deep
breath, biting back a smile at the sight of the bed – both
sides clearly slept in. She didn't really remember getting
there, but, if she tried hard enough, could still feel Cade's
arms around her.

That warmth carried her to the kitchen, the scene so
familiar from the day before that she had a sudden flash of
déjà vu. Cade was busy piling high a stack of pancakes on
a plate, a bottle of syrup next to them.

Izz slid onto a barstool. "Morning," she said quietly, trying to ignore the pounding in her head that was quickly intensifying in the bright morning light. A quick glance at the stove clock told her it was nearing noon.

"Morning," Cade replied just as softly, as though nervous. "How are you feeling?"

"Fine." She accepted the glass of orange juice he handed her, wondering at his hurried movements. He seemed agitated as he slapped the batter onto the frying pan. "Are you okay?"

"Fine." He didn't turn back around. He wanted to say he was fine with her, that he was elated she slept in his bed last night, but he wasn't fine with how he acted the night before. Nor was he fine with the worries that plagued him over *why* she moved in. For him? For her? Because she felt guilty? Because she really wanted to?

Izz watched the tension build in his shoulders. Clearly he wasn't *fine*, but was closing off, just like she was known to do. Now she knew just how annoying it was, her own frustration building as his did. "Are you mad that I moved my stuff in?"

"No."

"Are you upset about me drinking too much?"

"No."

With a huff, Izz reached out and grabbed a pancake from the plate. She stared at his back, now fully irritated, not willing to put this talk off any longer. So, she did the only thing that came to mind. She reared back her arm and released.

AT THE STOVE, CADE FLIPPED the last pancake, shut off the burner, and froze when something warm hit the back of his head. Glancing down, he saw a tattered pancake drop to his feet. He started to turn, ready to reprimand, but a second pancake followed, smacking him in the face. Izz stared across the counter at him, her expression a mix of satisfaction, annoyance, and amusement.

"Did you really just throw a pancake at me?"

She heard the pissy tone but ignored it. "Yeah, well, you were a dick last night. And you're being a dick now. Dicks get pancakes thrown at them."

"And what do insufferable chicken shits get thrown at them?" When her amusement turned quickly to one of warning, Cade picked up a piece of bacon and flicked it at her, hitting Izz squarely in the forehead.

"What the fuck did I do?" she cursed, hand reaching out for more ammo as she started to work her way around the counter.

"You refuse to let me in, Isabella."

Izz ducked as another piece of bacon flew her way. It bounced off her shoulder onto the floor. "I moved my stuff in last night! I thought that's what you wanted!"

"Is it what *you* want?"

Now thoroughly exasperated, Izz threw the pancake at him. It broke apart into several pieces mid-flight, and she took satisfaction in the fact that each one hit their mark. "Why do you have to question it? Stop being such a *girl*!"

He moved like lightning, catching her arm as she went to pelt him again and pushing her against the fridge. Instantly she reacted, shoving him away by his shoulders and muttering curses beneath her breath.

"You son of a bitch," she said up at him, not entirely sure why she was mad, but feeling like she should be. Her body moved against his, struggling to break free, arms and legs searching for something to connect with. Cade gripped her wrists and shoved them up over her head, where they would be of no danger to him. At the same time he pressed his knees between her legs, effectively trapping her between him and the fridge.

"Stop being such a pain in the ass *and listen to me!*" he yelled, surprising them both with his outburst. Izz stilled, fire in her eyes when she glared up at him. "I want every goddamn part of you, now and forever. I don't care how long we've known each other. I don't care that you make it your life's goal to make everything so fucking difficult. I don't even care that you make me work for it." He pressed himself closer, feeling the hard beat of her heart that betrayed the venom in her eyes. "But damn it, Isabella, I'm not taking this one step further until you say it."

Incredulous, Izz cocked her head and smirked. "I moved my stuff in–"

"I don't give a shit what you moved in," he interrupted, tightening his hold on her wrists when she made to move away. His head lowered, just inches from hers. "Just fucking say it."

She didn't want to give in, not to this brazen man who had the balls to hold her against a goddamn refrigerator like she was a rag doll, not to the familiar stranger who called her out on all her shit and made her own up to her fears. But then she felt it, that spark somewhere deep in her heart that told her no matter what she said, or didn't say, in this moment, she would never get Roarke Cadian out of her mind, body, or soul.

Eyes softening, mouth moving into the slightest of smiles, she whispered, "Maybe I do too."

It took him but a moment to realize the significance of her reply, a response to the words he'd thought went unheard last night. But that moment was all he needed before he crushed his lips to hers. He shifted her wrists to one hand, keeping her captive as the other hand trailed down her arm, grazed her breast, until finally it fisted in the center of her chest. With one rough tug, he ripped the ages-old tank away, leaving her in just her bra and sweats as she panted out her surprise.

"I liked that shirt." Her voice was heavy with lust.

"You'll like this better." His words sparked a fire between her legs.

Cade's mouth moved to her throat, curving into a grin against her skin at the taste of bacon grease lingering there. The feel of her heart beating had him nipping at the flesh, taking it between his teeth and biting down lightly, not enough to hurt, but enough to tear the breath out of her as she squirmed against him. His fingers inched their way to her back, deftly working the clasp of her bra until it sprung free. Only then did he release her wrists, yanking the material away from her body and lowering himself for a taste of the supple skin. Her hands found their way to his hair, pulling it free of its tie so the black locks fell across his shoulders. When her grip tightened, Cade pulled back, following the direction of her tugs until his mouth was back on hers.

Cade grunted when Izz worked a leg between them, her foot on his bare chest, pushing him back until he hit the counter. He stared across the small space, noting the playful glimmer in her eyes, the slightest hint of a smile.

Surging forward, he gripped her by the shoulders and dragged her to him, spinning so that she was against the counter, growling out her name when she turned, shoving him back in a dance of cat and mouse, laughing when his hands held firm to her waist and pushed her back against the fridge, trapping her once again right where he wanted her.

"Stay," he commanded, his voice husky and offering a promise that had her, for once, listening.

When he was sure she was staying put, Cade moved his hands from her waist and lower, his eyes never leaving hers as he slowly slid the pants over her hips, down her thighs, to her ankles, instantly hardening at the sight of her naked before him.

Izz shivered at the contrast of cold metal at her back and hot man at her front. Her fingers dug into muscle as Cade kissed her softly, lips lingering against hers as his hand slid down her stomach until his fingers touched the most sensitive parts of her. Then he was lowering himself to his knees, his mouth meeting his fingers.

Two fingers slid inside her, then three, as his tongue danced atop her clit to the symphony of her gasps. She felt hot breath and gentle teeth, teasing nips and long kisses, fingers sliding in and out until her knees weakened, but still he held her up. Izz wrapped his hair around her hands and held on for the ride, letting go of everything she'd kept bottled up inside, giving her body permission to respond as it longed to respond to the man taking pleasure in her pleasure. A glance down at Cade positioned between her legs, feasting on her body like his last meal, had her quivering even more until that spark in her heart grew, erupting throughout her body.

He caught her as she started to slide down the fridge. "Not yet, m'lady," he whispered. "I'm not done with you just yet."

Izz grinned lazily, a mischievous gleam in her eye. "Then take me," she replied, wrapping an arm around his neck. "Right here, as you wish."

With a hungry grunt matched by a flash of smirk, Cade spun Izz around, bending her over the kitchen counter until her stomach lay flat against the cold stone. With one hand he held her there by the back of the neck, with the other he shoved his jeans and boxers away, letting them fall to the floor. His feet pushed against hers until her legs were spread on either side of him and she was displayed before him, all wet, pink flesh and toned ass arched toward him in invitation. In one long, hard thrust he entered her, spurred on by the sound of her throaty moan.

He moved slowly at first, watching her every move, the way he slid in and out of her to the feel of her clenching against his shaft. His body betrayed his desire to treasure each slow push, urging him almost involuntarily to thrust harder and faster until their knees hit the cabinets. She was so wet and ready, he so hard and eager, that they became lost in the feel of being so wholly connected to one another.

One hand above her head, Izz kept up with his rhythm, using the two-tier counter for support as she met him thrust for thrust, forcing him deeper inside until his cock hit parts of her that exploded in an avalanche of shivers up her spine.

Her hips rotated in a way that had him gritting his teeth and biting back heady groans. Cade kicked out his feet, spreading her legs farther so that the angle of his pen-

etration changed, deepened, and he began to thrust upward, directing her body toward its ultimate pleasure.

When she glanced back at him over her shoulder, lips
parted, eyes narrowed in pleasure while her free hand
reached back to cup him, he lost all control and took her
from behind completely. His hands gripped her waist and
focused her ass against him, pound for pound, the slap of
skin against skin spurring him on until he emptied himself
inside her just as her name left his lips.

"Isabella," he whispered, leaning over so that his
chest touched her back. Her breathing matched hers as he
kissed her neck, her cheek, reluctant to move. "My Isabella."

Chapter 27

THEY SPENT THE DAY IN bed – their bed – talking and napping and eating the junk food Izz insisted he try. He wasn't much for sweets, but he succumbed to the double-fudge brownies she all but forced down his throat the first time, just as she succumbed to the local brew he insisted she try.

As morning wore on to afternoon, and afternoon to evening, Izz realized that this was where she was meant to be. Her life back in California wasn't one she could return to. She was contemplating where to go from there as she leaned over Cade, tracing the outline of the black tattoo spread across the center of his back and across his shoulders, down his right arm. The lines arched out from a spiral in the center, spinning into the shape of a sun tipped with reddish-orange flames.

"What does it mean?" she asked Cade as her fingers continued to work over his skin.

Lying on his stomach, Cade looked over at her, at the vision of a woman who had become completely his. "It's a symbol from my family's past," he answered breezily, watching her closely. "A reminder of where we came from, to always be brave, to remember the ones we fight for, and to be prepared for the trials we face in the future."

"What kind of trials?"

"The trials of our ancestors. Love, hate, conviction." He smiled when she leaned over and kissed the center of the tattoo, the darkest part of the sun. "My father always said that one day I would change the course for our family's fate. This mark was the reminder."

Izz stared down at the tattoo, thinking of her own father and the meaning of her ink. "My father said the same thing," she realized at the memory. "He used to draw this dragon, and said one day I would recognize it like part of my own soul, and know the part it plays in who we are." With a laugh, she nudged Cade's shoulder. "Maybe our dads knew each other in a past life."

He heard the humor in her words, but couldn't quite match her laugh. If only she knew how true her words might have been, he wondered as she dropped to her stomach, apparently done scrutinizing his back.

"Hungry?" he asked when he heard her stomach growl. At her sheepish smile, he rose and tugged on a pair of sweats. "I'll heat up some leftovers. Don't go anywhere. And don't get dressed," he added with a wink.

As his footsteps sounded down the hall, Izz flopped onto her back, thinking over the day. The perfect day, one she hadn't expected but treasured nonetheless. A buzzing to her right stopped any further introspection and she turned over, grabbing her phone from the nightstand.

We discussed this, Izz. You aren't supposed to be there.

"Asshole," she muttered. She'd thought this was over, that she took care of it back in California. A second message came through as she was trying to decide how to reply.

I gave you a chance. You didn't take it.

Rolling her eyes, Izz typed out, *Yeah? What are you gonna do about it?*

The answer came almost immediately. *You put their lives at risk. Their deaths will be on your hands.*

That had her pausing, fear creeping into her chest. "What?" she murmured, not sure how to take the answer.

"Something wrong?" Startled, Izz nearly dropped her phone. Cade saw the hesitation on her face. Before she could come up with an excuse, he pushed the subject. "Who are you talking to?"

"...I don't know," Izz said after a pause.

"Don't lie to me, Isabella."

"I'm not! And don't talk to me like I'm a child." Izz sat up and crossed her arms. "I really don't know who it is."

Still suspicious, Cade entered the room, hearing the beep of the microwave downstairs that told him the food was ready. "What's going on?"

Caught, Izz sighed and tossed him the phone. "This creep keeps texting me. It started when I was out here with the girls. I thought I'd taken care of it but I guess I was wrong."

Holding up a hand, Cade scrolled through the messages, anger building with each one. When he was finished, he handed her back the phone, crossing his arms. "What do you mean, you thought you took care of it?"

Her face scrunched up in distaste. "There is this guy back home, an old friend of my late husband. I don't know what Eric saw in the guy. He's a creep and a skeeze. But

191

anyway, he came on to me before we left and I wasn't exactly graceful about it. I guess this is his revenge."

"How did you take care of it?"

"Well … when I went home I marched into his office and told him to cut the shit."

Cade frowned. "And what did he say?"

"Well … he said he didn't like being threatened, basically."

"Isabella!"

Izz jumped up from the bed, the phone forgotten behind her. "What! I didn't think he'd start making death threats!" Suddenly sheepish, she clasped her hands together and chewed her bottom lip. "To be honest I'm not sure where to go from here."

The irrational, alpha male side of him said the next place to go was California to knock some guy's teeth in. But the rational side won out. "We go to the police," he answered, though his words were strained. "We've dealt with this kind of thing at *Quest*. Women who stalk the knights, want to be the damsel in distress. Usually it's harmless, if not creepy. But sometimes they threaten family, so the cops step in."

"But the number is blocked," Izz argued.

"So? You said you know who it is, so that's enough to go on. We'll go first thing in the morning."

When Izz nodded slowly, as though hesitant, Cade added, "Or I can fly out to California and deal with this guy myself."

Izz scoffed. "I don't need you fighting my battles like a caveman. I just don't know how he will respond."

Cade sat down next to her. "He responds how he responds. No matter what, you've got me."

Despite the seriousness of the threat, Izz smiled, warmth filling her as she leaned against him. She liked the sound of that.

THE NEXT DAY, CADE CARRIED through with his promise and brought Izz to the police station. By the end of the meeting she felt like all that would come of it would be one very pissed-off Bex, and one gigantic headache for her. Still, she went through with it because she knew it made Cade feel better, and she supposed the cops needed to know, just in case.

While she waited for the police to do their thing – which she guessed was serving Bex with some kind of 'quit being a tool and lay off the threatening texts' message – Izz got back to her work while Cade did the same. For Izz, work meant holing up in the den writing to the sound of Harry Potter battling dementors. For Cade, work meant checking in on the new guys as they prepared for their first show with the veterans. He was sitting out the first few shows, giving the others a chance to show off their new and practiced skills.

Upstairs, thoughts buried deep in her work, Izz almost didn't hear the doorbell ring. As it was, it took a few seconds for the sound to register, the writer fog in her head clearing enough for her to save her work and make her way downstairs. Part of her was frustrated by the interruption – she had a deadline, and an editor harping on her to meet it, not to mention the trip back to California he was insisting on. The other part was excited to see if she was right about who, or what, was at the door.

When she saw the delivery man on the front step, she

knew she was right. With a smile, Izz signed for the package then took it from him, brushing off his comments about its weight and hurrying inside. She brought the long, bulky box into the hallway, having to drag it the rest of the way to the living room. Once there, she tore it open until she was able to lift the top. A grin broke out when she saw what rested inside.

Her sword, her father's sword, shone up at her, glinting beneath the lights. Olivia had come through, packing and overnighting it at a moment's notice. It was the only time Izz had ever let any one of her friends touch the sword, and would likely be the last.

Pulling out the mounting materials, Izz began her search for tools, figuring they'd be in the garage. There she found a few drills and a box of heavy-duty nails, all she needed. She hoped Cade wouldn't mind her putting holes in the wall or her using his tools, but she'd become more than self-sufficient using them and didn't want to wait for him to get home. It certainly hadn't been her late husband making all those small home repairs.

Back in the living room, Izz approached the spot on the wall she'd always wondered about. That bare, empty spot that seemed to be waiting for the one piece to complete it, the piece she'd owned for more than half her life.

It was time to bring the two together.

Chapter 28

TOOLS IN HAND, IZZ MEASURED out the wall and sword mounting base, then felt along the wood for support beams. She'd learned the hard way what happened when she just drove a nail into a wall without seeing what was behind it first. A trip to the ER later, she was all the wiser about nails and studs.

Knocking on the wall, she listened for the telltale sign she needed, until her fingers drifted over the slightest catch in the wood. Pausing, Izz traced the catch, realizing it went in a perfectly shaped rectangle neatly hidden in the wall.

"Interesting," she muttered to herself, knowing that what she was about to do was an incredible invasion of privacy, but also not caring. Setting the drill down, she pushed and prodded at what she guessed was a hidden compartment in the wall until, finally, something clicked and a tray slid out.

"Awesome," she whispered, excitement curling in her gut as she lifted the gray cloth. She'd always wanted some sort of secret room, and was willing to settle for a secret hole in the wall. That excitement, though, turned to something close to dread when she saw the wooden box beneath it.

Her lips parted in surprise as she took in the designs. A man and woman mid-embrace, passionate lovers who couldn't live without one another. But that wasn't what caught her eye. It was the dragon on one side and the sun on the other, nearly exact replicas of her tattoo and Cade's, that had her heart skipping a beat. Shaky fingers touched the dragon first, the fierce creature her father used to draw, the one he'd promised she would recognize as part of her heart someday. Then they moved to the sun, the symbol of Cade's past that he could never forget, that which drove him to succeed, to be brave.

"It's not possible," Izz said, not sure if she was trying to convince herself or the ghosts of her parents. Her father had always hinted that they were descendants of the ones he loved to create stories about, had always gone into great detail about the maiden who lost her life to evil, teaching her how to look out for said evil should it ever return, but this … this was proof of the words she'd never truly believed.

Izz sucked in a quick, sharp breath when she touched the side of the box and something popped, then the top opened ever so slightly. Her hands trembled even more as they lifted the lid to reveal a velvet-lined interior with something resting atop.

Taking a moment to catch her breath, Izz slowly inched forward until she could see inside.

And in that box was a prophecy. Bits of the story floated through her mind. Some part of her had always imagined it was a piece of paper with a promise of the future scrawled across, but there was no paper. Just the trinket, a beautiful necklace with a red stone pendant that shimmered beneath the light. Lifting it from the box, Izz almost shuddered at the feel of the cold stone against her fingers. She turned it over. On the back was an engraving in a language she didn't understand, but could guess at what it said. Something about two souls reuniting in the distant future, each with a piece of one another to make a whole.

Swallowing hard, Izz put everything back and closed the box, setting it back in the wall. Once the compartment was hidden again, her fear and anxiety turned to rage. Rage for never fully knowing the truth, rage for having to discover her heritage this way, rage for the person who clearly knew and was hiding everything from her all along.

That fury spurred her into action, putting the box back in the wall and shoving her sword under the couch temporarily, then driving with blind purpose to *Quest for Avalon,* She stomped in through the employee entrance and followed the sounds of male laughter. She found them, all of them, surrounding one of the sparring pits, cheering on two men in the center.

Cade was one of those men, broadsword in one hand, shield strapped to the other. He and another man with long, curly hair danced around the circle, sweat dripping down their faces. Their chests were wrapped in sparring armor, as were their thighs. Izz barely saw any of it as she stalked up to the ring, grabbed a shield and sword leaning against the railing, and entered to shouted protests behind her.

Cade and the other man heard the yells and broke free of their sparring. That hesitation was all Izz needed to shove the newcomer to the side and slam her shielded arm against Cade, who stumbled back a few steps.

"You goddamn sneaky sack of bullshit," she snarled at him, hitting his shield with hers again. "When were you going to tell me? When!"

His arm lifted in automatic defense when she launched into attack mode. Metal sparked against metal as they sparred, one in anger and one in utter confusion. When he finally got a handle on the fight, Cade backed up, out of sword's reach. "You mind telling me what the hell this is about?"

"Oh, I don't know. Maybe the secret box you didn't feel the need to tell me about." At Cade's pause, Izz nodded. "Yeah, that's what I thought." She pushed forward, countering his parrying, raising her shield when he went on the offense. All the while, she continued to accuse him, desperate to get the torturous thoughts out of her mind.

"Is any of this even real? Is it just some bullshit attempt at *fate*?" she said the word like it tasted bad. "Do you even give a shit or are you just trying to fulfill a *story*?"

The guys cheered when she advanced, her moves accented with such skill and strength that Cade was as impressed as he was worried. Her eyes burned with both fury and concentration. It wasn't hard to block her attacks, as he was every bit as skilled and that much larger, but he was growing weary of being forced into a fight with no idea as to why.

"Were you ever going to tell me? Were you ever going to give me a choice?" Izz spun when his sword reached for her stomach. Panting, she glared across the pit at him. "Or did you just play me for a fool?"

At that, Cade threw his sword to the sand and risked the four steps over to her, grabbing her wrist and forcing her arm out to her side so the weapon was of no matter to him. He lowered his head so only she could hear the words growled into her ear. "Everything I feel for you is real, Isabella. You know that."

When she struggled, he only tightened his hold. "I can explain everything, if you'll stop trying to cut my head off. Can we discuss this like rational adults?"

Fire burned in her eyes when she cocked her head up to stare at him. Her jaw set, Cade recognized the look a second too late and her knee slammed into his, causing his leg to buckle. He fell to his back and her sword followed, pointing at his throat as the guys catcalled and laughed.

"You have ten minutes," she told him, then threw sword and shield to the side before stalking out of the pit.

SHE WAITED IN THE MAIN arena, sitting on top of the railing overlooking the sand. The smell of horses lingered in the air, one she was starting to love, as it reminded her of Cade. Even if she was mad at him right now, that scent still did strange things to her insides.

Footsteps behind her had her thoughts shifting, and she let out a deep breath when Cade took a seat next to her, their legs dangling over the edge. "Sorry for the wait," he said after a pause. "The guys were razzing me about being beaten by a girl."

Despite herself, Izz smiled, ducking her head so he wouldn't see. "Serves you right."

"Maybe." When Izz looked up at him, brow furrowed, he merely lifted a shoulder. "Would you have ever agreed to a date if I told you I thought you were destined to be with me because a prophecy from the medieval era told me so?"

Thinking about that scenario, Izz frowned. "No," she admitted. "But you had plenty of chances after. I told you about my family, and all my father's stories. You acted like it was all brand-new information."

"I didn't want to scare you off. For what it's worth, I didn't know who you were when we met. Your friends asked me to be nice to you and I thought that was it. When I saw you, I thought you were a beautiful woman and it would be an honor to make you smile. When I met you, and touched your hand, I felt something."

Izz scoffed. "What, the desire to get in my pants?"

Cade couldn't help but chuckle. "Well, yes. But later I realized it was more than just instant attraction. You felt … right, like you were the one I was waiting for all this time. When you told me about your father's stories, I knew I was right."

"Right about what?"

"That destiny had finally caught up with us."

Running her hands through her hair, Izz jumped off the railing into the sand, starting to pace. "Cade, this kind of thing, it's not possible. I write about fantasy and magic, but it's not real! I mean, you're telling me that … that this tattoo I have on my back is some thousand-year-old desire to be reunited with my knight in shining armor, and the tattoo on your back is the reminder of your lost love? But this stuff doesn't exist in this real world!"

"What if it does?" Cade leapt down next to her. "I didn't believe it when I was younger either, but eventually I came to realize that sometimes you just have to accept what is. Some things were put in place far before our time, during an age where things happened that we just can't understand. What if you let yourself believe, just for a second, that it could be real?"

The fears she didn't want to voice bubbled to the surface, along with fresh tears. Izz swallowed hard, avoiding his gaze. "Then … then it means I married the wrong man, and that he died because of me."

"Isabella, no–"

"Don't." She held up a hand. "Look, I get why you didn't tell me. Yeah, I was mad, but I'm calm now. I won't try to stab you with a sword anymore." She could only frown at the sad smile he tried to hide. "But I need to process this. I have to think about some things."

"I'll go with you," he said automatically, turning as though to run grab his things.

"No, Cade. I need to be alone. I just need to think."

His eyes looked hurt, but he nodded. "Will I see you at home?"

The worry in his voice put an ache deep in her heart. "Yes," she promised, turning to leave. Just as she reached the doorway, she looked back at Cade, who was watching her, hands in his pockets, looking entirely forlorn. "Will you wait up for me?"

The tension eased from his shoulders as he smiled. "Until the stars no longer shine, m'lady."

Chapter 29

THE BEACH WAS MOSTLY EMPTY as Izz walked along the shoreline for over an hour, for once enjoying the way the water splashed over her bare feet. Her head ached with the possibilities placed before her. On the one hand, she was thrilled by the idea of a prophecy foretelling a fate written in the pages of history. On the other, she hated the thought of not having a choice, and that choosing wrong had led to a good man's death.

"It's not real," she whispered, struggling to accept that the fantastical concepts she wrote about could be true. She kicked at the sand. "Magic doesn't exist. I make my own goddamn destiny."

But she wanted it to be real. More than anything, she wanted Cade to be hers in a way that had them bonded over thousands of years.

She thought about all the stories her father had told her. The knight was a brave and fierce man, yet devoted to his family and known to be just as charming as he was deadly. The maiden was fair and kind, but with a wild edge that captured the knight's interest at first glance. And the evil that drove them apart was just that, a dark force that hid itself well behind a trickster's mask.

Izz had often wondered which, if any, of the three sides of the triangle her family defined, though her father always made sure to pay special care to the maiden's details. She'd always just assumed he fancied the woman in a fairy tale he'd come to know by heart.

In her hand, her phone vibrated. Still dazed, Izz didn't think twice about swiping the screen, then grimaced at the message.

The rope you walk is fraying. The choices you make will be your end.

Izz sighed, not in the mood to deal with this bullshit. Most days she loved technology. Tonight, she could do without it. *Why the fuck do you even care?*

It is who we are, dear Isabella. Evil lurks in one of our hearts.

The reply made her stop, nearly tripping over her own feet. Suddenly she wasn't so sure this was about unrequited love, or lust rather, after all.

You have three days to return to California, the message chirped.

Izz rolled her eyes. *Or what?* The worst Bex could do was, what? Burn her house down? She already had everything that mattered to her in Myrtle Beach. She didn't think he would go that far though. He may have been a creep, but she was about ninety-nine percent he was all talk and no bite.

Or you'll know what happens when you don't listen to me.

If you say so. She meant it sarcastically and wondered how the answer was received. Deciding she didn't care, and that maybe another trip to the police station was in order, Izz turned around and headed home. She wasn't any closer to a resolution to her thoughts, but she was willing to talk things through, figure out what destiny had in store for her after all.

Cade was waiting for her when she arrived, stepping out of the living room at the sound of the back door opening. The relief in his smile and the strength of his embrace as he wrapped his arms around her told Izz she'd made the right decision. This was where she belonged now, and no one could take that away from her.

SHE SPENT THE NEXT FEW days working, blissfully left alone by Bex the Stalker, to the point that she all but forgot about him. By the end of the week she had her rough draft completed and emailed to the editor to prove she actually was listening to him when he demanded proof of progress.

Taking a break from the first round of edits, Izz stood up and stretched, picking up the empty cans and wrappers surrounding her. The amount of junk food she'd consumed recently probably should have concerned her, and did enough to convince her to take a run down the beach. At one time she'd actually enjoyed exercise, especially running, but that hobby fell by the wayside in the past year.

Deciding it was time to take back that part of her life, Izz rummaged through the closet for her running shoes, coming up empty. Her searches through the few bags she hadn't yet unpacked also yielded nothing but random shit she didn't need at the moment. "Figures," she said to herself, pulling her phone from her pocket and dialing Olivia's number.

Her friend picked up almost immediately. "Thought you fell off the face of the planet."

"Love you too, Liv," Izz replied dryly. "So, how much do you love me?"

She heard her friend sigh good-naturedly. "What do you want?"

"My running shoes." Izz rolled her eyes when Olivia snorted. "Seriously! It's time I get back into running, but I think I forgot my shoes, the nice running ones I bought a couple years ago. Can you ship them to me?"

"Seriously? Why don't you just go buy new ones?"

"Because, those are all nice and broken in."

Olivia sighed an exaggerated sigh. "Fine. I'll swing by now since I'm on my way home. But we both know you're only asking to get out of actually exercising."

"Awesome, thanks. And yeah, you're probably right. So," Izz continued, abandoning her own search and heading downstairs for a drink, "how's things? How are the girls?"

"Oh, same old girls," Olivia answered breezily, the noise of cars honking sounding behind her. "The twins are doing their twin thing. I think they are planning some camping trip with the husbands. Haven't heard from Miley in about a week. Last we talked, she met some fling of the week and was planning on shacking up with him. You know Miley."

"Yes, I do," Izz laughed. "So, how's D?"

There was a pause before Olivia answered. "She's good. She's still chatting it up with that hot knight. I think she really likes him … She thinks you're still mad at her."

Izz made a face, even though her friend couldn't see it. "I'm not mad. I was annoyed, but I'm over it."

"I know, and you have every right to be. Just know that she has your best interests at heart. Okay," she changed the subject. "I'm at your house. Going to get these shoes and get home. I'm starving, I hope you know."

With a laugh, Izz walked out to the back deck and stared out at the water. "Yeah, yeah. My guess is they are in my bedroom closet."

"Sweet, maybe I'll borrow something you so kindly left behind," Olivia teased. "Okay, I'm in. Heading to the bedroom. By the way, your house smells weird."

"Yeah well, I haven't been home in a while. Things get stale."

"I'll say. Okay, up the stairs, in your room, checking out your closet. Ooh, I like this red dress. I'm gonna borrow it."

"Focus, Liv," Izz said with another chuckle, knowing it would be a good six month before she ever saw that dress again. "Running shoes. Bright blue with neon green laces."

"Not too concerned about style, huh?"

"Shut up."

"I don't see them, Izz. Are you sure you didn't bring them?"

Izz turned away from the water and headed back inside, into the den where the rest of her items were stored in boxes. "Yeah, pretty sure. Check the office. Sometimes things get left in there when I'm working," she suggested as she rummaged through the boxes.

"Ugh, the office," Olivia complained. "It's like a hoarder's heaven in there." But Izz heard her trudging down the hall anyway. "The smell is stronger here. I told you your house smells weird."

Izz shrugged to herself. "Maybe I left some food out. Wouldn't be the first time."

"No kidding," Olivia muttered. "Okay. In the office, check. Scanning the world's messiest floor for ugly shoes. Seriously, girl, it's called a trash can. Use it."

"Just look for the shoes."

"I am. Checking the desk area, couch, nope. Checking the closet. I ... wait." When Olivia stopped speaking, Izz paused. "What the hell is that?"

"What the hell is what?"

"It's like a ... Oh my God. Oh my God. Holy shit. I'm gonna—I can't—"

Her words ended on a scream, a high-pitched wail that startled Izz so badly that she fell backward. Catching herself, hearing Olivia all but losing her mind on the other end of the phone, Izz fought to catch her attention. "Olivia! Olivia! *Liv*! What is it? What did you find? Talk to me, goddamn it!"

Olivia's sobs echoed through the line. "I saw ... I saw red. Red hair." She took a gulping breath and tears formed in Izz's eyes, knowing what was coming next. "Jesus fucking Christ. Miley. It's *Miley*, Izz! What the fuck is she doing in your closet? *What the fuck is going on*?!"

A tear fell down her cheek, bile rising in the back of her throat. "What ... what happened, Liv?" she asked on a whisper, her voice a croak. "What happened to Miley?"

"She ... she's *dead*, Izz!" Olivia shouted, her words cracking. "I can't ... What do I do? Holy shit. I'm going to pass out."

"No. Olivia, stay with me. Just ... go to the front door and wait. I'll call the police. Stay on the line with me, okay? Talk to me. Just keep talking to me."

Izz stumbled from the den, the hallway blurring and twisting as she tried to make her way downstairs, functioning on adrenaline alone. She had to stay calm. She had to take care of Olivia. She had to call the police. She had to help Miley.

But first she had to get to the kitchen.

Nearly tripping over her feet as she entered, still demanding to Olivia to keep talking, Izz picked up the only landline in the house and frantically dialed, not even sure what she was saying to the operator on the other end. All she would remember later was the man's voice who picked up, the blur of her words shouted at him to get to her house, and the sound of her sobs mixing with Olivia's.

30

IZZ SAT HUNCHED OVER, ELBOWS resting on her knees and head hung low, as the world rushed on around her. At some point she felt a warm hand on her back, heard a low voice speaking softly in her ear, but Izz couldn't process any of it. All her mind's eye knew were those ten minutes of Olivia screaming, crying, begging for someone to help, all while knowing help was too late. Izz hadn't even witnessed the scene firsthand, but she didn't need to. The pain and shock in her friend's voice were enough.

"Isabella," Cade whispered, kneeling in front of her and placing his hands on her legs. "You need to speak with the police. They need to do their job and figure out who..." His voice trailed off, but she knew what came next.

Who killed Miley.

One deep, shuddering breath later, Izz nodded and straightened enough to look the officer in the eye. His expression was soft, sympathetic, as he stepped closer to the couch she was resting on and took a seat on the edge of the coffee table in front of her and Cade.

"Ms. Nevear, we just need to go over a few things."

When Izz nodded, he continued. "Can you walk me through what happened, up to speaking with the officer in California?"

Sniffling, Izz told him everything she knew, from the search for her shoes to Olivia rummaging through her house to the cops showing up on the other end of the line to let her know they were there and had the situation under control. "Olivia said the house smelled weird. I thought I just left food out and it was rotting or something," Izz said, ungracefully wiping her nose with the back of her hand. "She just started screaming … I've never heard her make that sound."

Though the emotion showed on his face, the officer didn't comment and instead turned the conversation back to the facts. "On the phone, before Ms. Olivia Candor arrived at your house, what did you discuss?"

She struggled to remember. It seemed so long ago. "Um … we talked about the girls. I missed them. She said Miley," her voice broke on the name, "had met some guy and wanted to shack up with him. She said she hadn't heard from her in about a week."

"Do you know who the man was?"

"No." Izz shook her head. "But that's not uncommon. Miley has her flings, gets them out of the way, and then we hear about it later."

The officer wrote down a note. "Can you think of anyone who would want to hurt Miley, or you? Someone who might be trying to send you a message?"

The question brought Izz out of her haze. Her lips parted and mentally she cursed herself for being so god-damn stupid. "Bex."

Both the officer and Cade frowned at her nearly silent

reply. "What?" they asked in unison.

"Breckan Bex," Izz replied, louder this time. "I filed a report with the police recently due to some harassing text messages. I got a few more messages about a week ago." At Cade's sudden jerk of surprise and accusatory glare, Izz held up her hands. "I'm sorry I didn't tell you. I thought he was just being a jerk and ignored him, and then I just forgot." She pulled out her phone and handed it to the officer, who scrolled through the messages.

"Seems this anonymous texter thought you would listen and return home. You staying here wasn't expected, nor was your friend being the one to find the body."

The body. The words sent a fresh wave of tears through Izz. It was her fault Miley was dead. She should have listened, should have gone home, should have taken the messages more seriously. Although, she had a feeling that even if she had returned, Miley would still be dead, and maybe Izz along with her.

"What happens now?" Cade asked, sliding an arm around her shoulders and pulling her closer to him.

The officer sighed and straightened. "I'll finish up the report and look into your report with Mr. Bex. I'll make sure the police on the other end know he is a suspect. You will likely need to make a trip back home, Ms. Nevear."

After a few more formalities were exchanged, the police left, Cade and Izz now alone to face their thoughts. Cade saw the officers out before returning to the couch, where Izz had laid down, head resting on a pillow, red eyes staring vacantly at the wall.

He sat down next to her, rubbing her back. "Isabella–"

"Can you not lecture me right now?" she cut in, her

tone defeated. "I know what I should have done. I know what's my fault. Can you just … not."

"I wasn't going to lecture you," Cade replied honestly, at a loss for what to say or do. "Just tell me what you need, Isabella."

She didn't know what she needed. All she knew was the feel of this couch, and the feel of the ache in her heart.

CADE MADE THE PLANS IN her stead, booking a flight out to the west coast at the request of the sheriff in California handling Miley's murder. Despite Izz's protests, he bought a ticket for himself, too, leaving *Quest* in the hands of the manager for a few days.

The night before the flight, Cade packed their bags. A quick glance through hers satisfied Izz. She barely slept that night, choosing instead to spend the evening and early-morning hours browsing the Internet, reading the latest articles about Miley, looking at the only picture of the crime scene that had been released, seeing photos of her home's exterior that cast the house in an eerie shadow, attempting to research Bex but finding nothing on the man.

The flight went smoothly, Izz staring out the window, Cade taking her hand when he saw the tears forming in the corners of her eyes. After picking up their bags and securing the rental car, Cade drove away from the airport, following the GPS to her house. In the meantime, Izz sent a text to Olivia, letting her know she was back in town.

The closer they got to her residence, the more nervous Izz became. She hadn't been back since her impulse return to Myrtle Beach, but she didn't miss this house or have any desire to go inside. Just the sight of it made her uncomfortable, unwelcome. They sat in the driveway for a few minutes, both staring up at the beautiful home shadowed by yellow police tape draping across the ground. Izz already knew that she had clearance to return, but she wasn't sure what to expect inside.

With a sigh, she dragged herself out of the car and trudged up the front steps, letting herself in. The house smelled stale and dirty, a mix of death and too many people going in and out during the investigation. Mud was caked on the floor in some places, while pieces of trash lined the kitchen counter. Ignoring it all, Izz walked through the kitchen and past the living room, up the stairs to the one place she didn't want to go but knew she had to see.

Her feet froze in the doorway to the office, rooted firmly on the hardwood. Izz swallowed painfully, glancing down at the yellow tape hanging from the frame that looked like it had been quickly torn down but not fully cleaned up, then into the office. From her vantage point everything seemed completely normal. The usual mess was spread across the floor, the desk covered in random pieces of paper with notes and ideas scribbled across them, the couch layered in blankets, the TV remote likely buried beneath one of them. And, in the far corner, the closet.

Forcing herself to move, Izz entered the room, slowly wading through the mess. Her hand shook as she reached out for the sliding door, throat constricting as she pushed it aside. Izz dropped to her knees with a sniffle when the door slid open. Her eyes latched on to a spot on the floor, one single spot stained a darker color than the rest, a spot that the police hadn't been able to clean – or perhaps didn't even try to. Miley's neck had been broken, the police reported, but she'd also sustained what appeared to be a knife wound to the back.

In her mind, Izz imagined Olivia in this same position, looking through the boxes shoved on the right side while chatting aimlessly, turning her gaze to the left, seeing a mass of red hair and then … the body attached to it. A chill worked its way through Izz.

"I'm sorry, Miley," she whispered, as though the ghost of her friend still lingered in the dark room. "I'm sorry I wasn't here. I'm sorry I could have saved you, but was too stupid to listen."

"It wasn't your fault."

The voice wasn't one she expected to hear. Izz glanced over her shoulder to see Deanna standing in the middle of the room, hands clutched in front of each other, eyes trying to look anywhere but the closet.

"D?"

"Olivia is in the car. She … she didn't think she could come inside," Deanna explained softly. "Cade is on the front porch. I said I'd find you. I figured you'd be in here."

Izz's attention returned to the closet as sadness overwhelmed her. "It was my fault," she replied. "If I'd been here, none of this would have happened."

"You can't blame yourself for the actions of some crazy, sick fuck, Izz. If you'd been here, it probably would have been you."

"And that makes it better?" she snapped.

Deanna held out her hands. "No, I'm sorry, I didn't mean it like that. I just mean … you couldn't have predicted what would happen, and no matter what you did, someone probably would have died."

The words failed to comfort her, instead only fueling

her rage-induced grief. Izz forced back her tears and rose to her feet. With a single nod, she approached her friend. "I should go see how Liv is doing."

Deanna led her out of the house, their arms linked in a familiar way that reminded Izz of their many years of friendship. She waited patiently while Izz locked the door, then walked her to the car, Cade following behind. Once there, Izz paused, seeing Olivia sitting in the back. Knowing what her friend wanted, and needed, she slid in the backseat next to her, Cade taking the front passenger side.

As Deanna started the car, Izz looked over at Olivia. "I'm sorry," she whispered again, this time for a different reason. Olivia seemed to understand, but didn't reply, instead resting her head on her friend's shoulder, both of them taking comfort in the gesture.

Chapter

32

THE OTHERS WERE WAITING FOR them when they arrived at Olivia's apartment. Beth and Jackie stood up from their spot on the bottom stair, hugging Izz tightly when she approached. Their husbands hung back, introducing themselves to Cade after he came to a stop behind Izz. A somber cloud hung over them, no one really wanting to talk, everyone wishing they could go back in time to a happier day.

Once the girls were settled in the living room and the men in the kitchen, Izz began the conversation she didn't want to have. "Tell me everything you know."

Olivia didn't respond, and Deanna seemed reluctant, so Beth took over. "The investigation is still going on. After ... after you spoke with the cops that day, they brought in Olivia, then us three," she gestured to her sister and Deanna, "to see what we knew about Miley. Where she may have been, who she was talking to. I don't know that any of us really knew anything. You know how Miley is ... was," Beth corrected herself with a sniffle. Izz did know – their departed friend was impulsive and rash. No one could ever keep up with her.

"They did a big investigation with your house, which I'm sure you already know about. I don't know the right terms. You know, looking for fingerprints, trying to figure out why the alarm didn't go off, checking for footprints, any clues." Beth gripped Jackie's hand for strength and support. "Miley ... they said she was stabbed first. But it didn't look like there was any other sign of trouble, like she fought the person or anything."

Even knowing most of the details already, Izz frowned over that, a thought forming in the back of her mind. Why wouldn't Miley fight? Was she taken by surprise, stabbed in the back before she even knew danger was lurking? Was she stabbed before she saw the person? Or, perhaps, did she know her killer, and hadn't been expecting an attack?

"The police don't have any leads," Jackie put in, and Izz's head snapped up at that.

"What about Bex?" When the girls all exchanged glances, she clenched her fists in response. "What aren't you telling me?"

Jackie held up a hand. "Don't get mad. But ... Bex isn't in jail. They brought him in for questioning, but released him."

Izz leapt to her feet. "Are you fucking kidding me? *How* is that possible?"

"He had an alibi," Deanna said from her side. "They wouldn't tell us what it was, just that he had one."

"Oh really," Izz said to herself, steeling her nerves. "Well, maybe I'll go ask him myself."

With that she snatched Olivia's keys off the table and stormed out, ignoring her friends yelling behind her and Cade's demand that she stop. She knew they would follow, which was fine. She only needed a few minutes' head start anyway.

When she arrived at the office, she wasn't surprised to see the parking lot mostly empty. Being brought in for questioning on a murder charge was bad for business. Izz slammed through the front door, sending one look at the receptionist that warned her of what would happen should she try to stop her.

Bex must have seen her coming, because he was already standing when she barged into his office. He held up a hand. "Izz–"

"You shut the fuck up, you son of a bitch." She stalked up and shoved him hard against the bookshelf behind his desk. His back hit the wood and he winced, but she wasn't done. Her fist connected with his chin before he even saw her move. "I don't know how you did it, or how you got away with it, but I swear to God I will make you pay every day for the rest of your life!"

"Izz!" He was shouting now, fighting back against her fists, but not fighting her. "Calm the fuck down!"

"Calm down?" she repeated incredulously as he wiped at the blood on his lip. "*Calm down*? After what you did?" She grabbed hold of the sharpest thing she could see on his desk, a pair of scissors, and held them against his throat. He stilled instantly, glaring down at her. "Tell me why."

Bex arched his neck, which succeeded only in making the metal dig in deeper. "I didn't kill her, Izz," he said carefully. "The police know that. I have an alibi."

"Then what the fuck is it." It wasn't a question, but a demand.

"You won't like it."

"I won't ask again."

Bex winced again when she pushed harder. "Okay, okay. I was here, then the florist, then a restaurant."

Confused, Izz lowered the scissors, but only a little. "You were on a date? Why wouldn't I like that? I don't give a shit about your love life."

He hesitated. "I was waiting for Miley."

The confusion spread, turning to ice in her veins. Her arm locked in place, her only defense against her would-be stalker. "Explain."

Bex, seeming to notice her wavering front, relaxed just a bit. "I saw Olivia and Miley at your house."

"Why the hell were you at my house."

The growl that emanated from her throat nearly terrified him. In his panic, though, he was surprised to hear she didn't know of his visit. "I went to talk some sense into you, tell you to keep your ass out of my office. They were there. Miley had found out about your threatening texts and told me to knock it off. She was yelling and pointing her finger at me, and looked beautiful doing it. So I asked her on a date."

"She would never say yes."

"You're right," Bex agreed. "She laughed in my face. So … I found her online and sent her a message asking her out again, the next day. She said yes."

"That doesn't make any sense," Izz argued. "Why would she go out with you if she knew you were being such a creep?"

"I told her I'd stop texting you if she went on one date."

The scissors resumed their place against his throat. "You told me you didn't send them."

"I know. And I didn't. I lied to her so she'd agree." When Izz's jaw clenched, he quickly continued. "We met at this little diner down the road. She said she showed up, so I had to stop. It was then I told her I wasn't really the stalker, but I just wanted to see her again. For whatever reason, she stayed." He dared a swallow when her hand wavered. "We kept seeing each other, a few times a day. Mostly grabbing a bite to eat, or going to the movies. I was waiting for her the night she ... the night she was killed. That was my alibi. People could place me at each location at specific times. They knew I couldn't have done it."

Almost completely defeated and entirely lost, Izz dropped her arm but remained close enough to attack again. "If she knew, or at least thought, that you weren't behind it, why wouldn't she tell me?"

Bex nearly smirked at her. "You and I aren't exactly on friendly terms, Izz. What would have happened if she told you she was dating me?"

A thousand thoughts raced through her mind, forcing Izz back a few steps until she dropped into one of the chairs by his desk. The scissors fell to the floor, forgotten, as she leaned over and buried her head in her hands. She wanted to be angry, to blame him, blame *someone*, for Miley's murder, but the energy had fled her body.

"Did you kill my friend, Bex?" she whispered.

At that, Bex slumped, though she didn't see the change in his posture, which was usually so refined. "I was falling in love with her," was his quiet response.

Izz looked up at him, surprised by the pain in his voice and on his face. Despite her hate for the man, she sensed his answer to be true. "Yes or no, Bex."

"Of course not, Izz," he said, somewhat angrily. "We

may not get along, but do you really think I'm a murderer? I wanted to be with Miley. Build something together. I didn't kill her."

A hollow pain filled her chest as Izz rose to her feet. "Then who did?"

"YOU BELIEVE HIM."

Izz toyed with her hands as Cade closed the door and sat in the chair across from her. They'd opted for a hotel room rather than Izz's house, as she didn't want to sleep in the room next to where her friend's body had been stashed. All of the girls had offered for her and Cade to stay with them, but she needed to be alone.

Cade and Deanna had showed up at Bex's office to fetch her, agreeing to leave peacefully at her insistence. Not long after, Izz said her goodbyes for the day, needing to get away from everyone, having only enough energy to call her editor and get his usual room at a nearby hotel where he came into town on business. It was a bit fancier than she typically preferred, but much better than the alternative.

"I do," Izz replied reluctantly. "You should have seen the look on his face. I've known Bex a long time. He's smooth, but he's not that smooth a liar."

"Just an asshole."

"Yeah, just an asshole," Izz sighed, running her hands through her hair. "I don't understand why Miley would have been seeing him, of all people, knowing everything she knew about him."

"People do stupid things."

"Apparently," Izz muttered. She couldn't deny that

Bex was attractive, certainly the type Mile had gone for, but he was such a creep that it didn't matter. Though, the more she thought about it, she supposed that her opinion was tarnished by the fact that she simply didn't like him. He'd never done anything overtly bad to her outside of snide comments and attempting to drag her late husband to strip clubs every time she was out of town. And, of course, hitting on her. To her friends, he likely appeared to be just another cocky, well-off man more interested in bedpost notches than meaningful relationships.

In other words, a male version of Miley.

Tired of the conversation, she started getting ready for bed, Cade following her lead. Once they were both tucked beneath the sheets and comforter, which Izz noted were much nicer than her own, silence befell them.

Izz stared up at the ceiling, contemplating the past few months, amazed at where she'd been and where she was now. Some of it was a good amazement – having met a great guy, possibly being able to love him, though she refused to admit it was because of some twist of fate. Some of it was bad – a crazy person texting her, losing one of her best friends.

For Cade, there was no question that he was falling in love with this woman lying next to him. He'd known the moment he saw her that she was special, and it wasn't just fate making him feel that way. It was real, pure, waiting-for-a-lifetime love that would only build and strengthen over time. And now, he worried he would lose it. One person was already dead, and he feared Izz would be next. He knew she took the threat seriously, but also knew that she would likely try to face it head on and alone, running straight onto the battlefield to fight her own wars.

"I'm going to sell my house," Izz said suddenly, breaking them both out of their reverie. Cade looked over at her, but her stare was fixed on the ceiling. "There are a lot of memories there, really good and really bad. I just … I don't think the good memories outweigh the bad anymore. It's time to let it go."

Sadness and regret filled her voice. Cade rolled onto his side, propping his head up with his hand and gazing down at her. "What then?"

She knew what he was asking, what he wanted to hear, but wasn't sure she had the energy to face that right now. "Then … I don't know. Can we deal with that when it comes?"

"One step at a time," he promised, brushing a strand of hair from her forehead before leaning over and kissing her softly. Izz accepted the kiss, wrapping her arms around him when he rolled on top of her. They made love softly, gently, that night, one tender moment after another that made her feel, finally, that maybe she wasn't alone in this after all.

IZZ DID HER DUTY FOR her friend over the next few days, meeting with enough police offers to lose count and telling her story enough times to be sick of the sound of her own voice. And, by the end of it all, they were no closer to solving the case than before.

She spoke with Miley's family about the funeral arrangements, offering much-needed money to cover the costs, as she knew her friend's parents struggled with their own bills, let alone any added expenses. Cade she sent home, insisting that he get back to work while she tied up the loose ends, promising that she had pulled herself together enough to do so.

In front of the girls, she tried her best to appear as unbroken as possible. They were expecting her to crumble and she couldn't afford to do that. Not anymore. This time, she had to be the strong one, especially for Olivia.

Izz sat next to her on the couch now, their knees touching. "Did you talk to that doctor?" she asked, referring to the specialist one of the officers had recommended after seeing the effect finding Miley's body had on Olivia.

The other woman nodded, the movement slow and

lifeless. Her formerly bright eyes were dull, tired. "He was nice. He listened, offered some advice. I'm going back in a couple days."

"Is there anything I can do?"

Olivia took in a deep breath. Letting it out slowly, she nodded again, this time looking over at Izz. "Yeah. You can find the mother fucker who did this. He wants you, Izz. Not any of us. The cops clearly can't help. Bex insists it's not him and for the most part we all believe him. So, it's up to you." She regarded Izz with a steely stare. "Maybe he'll come after us, maybe he won't. But I have a feeling it's coming down to a final fight soon and you have to be ready. You have to figure out exactly what he wants, and end him. Just fucking end him."

The truth of her reply hit Izz hard in the chest. She heard the accusations beneath the words, the same ones she'd already bestowed upon herself. Shifting uncomfortably, she nodded. "I will, Liv. I promise."

"Good." Olivia bit back a fresh wave of tears. "Because I can't bury you too."

They parted ways soon after, Olivia to get some rest and Izz to finish finalizing plans for her move to South Carolina. She hadn't told her friends yet. Only Cade and her real estate agent knew that she was leaving California behind, and doing so meant starting the long job of packing up her house.

Her home was dark, too dark, foreboding in its silence. Izz went around turning on every light she could, only somewhat relieved by the light that cast away the shadows. For a moment she considered calling Cade, but knew doing so would only put him on the next flight back to California, and she didn't want that. She didn't want anyone taking care of her right now.

Some things she had to do on her own.

Resigned to the fact that she wasn't going to get much, if any, sleep that night, Izz started the packing process. She'd already called movers and arranged for them to pack up what she didn't ship to South Carolina within the next week. It would all go in storage until she could figure out what to do with it. The house she would put on the market as soon as the police gave her the go-ahead. She wasn't sure who would want to buy a house where a dead body was found, but figured it would go eventually.

She started in the living room, wrapping pictures of her parents, her friends, and Eric. She didn't know the proper protocol for keeping pictures of a late husband when there was a new man sharing her bed, but Izz wasn't yet willing to part with all of her memories just yet.

Two hours later she moved to the kitchen, finding herself packing only the things she knew Cade didn't have. Refusing to think about what that meant, Izz soldiered through, taking quick breaks here and there to grab a snack and drink. By the time she was ready to move upstairs, it was nearing two in the morning. She bypassed the office and went straight to her bedroom, starting with her clothes, tossing a bunch into a pile to give to Olivia.

When her closet and dresser were emptied, Izz turned to the second dresser, the one she hadn't touched in over a year. Her friends, and her former in-laws, had been on her for a long time to clean out Eric's personal belongings, but she hadn't had the heart to do so. It took her a moment to gather the courage to open the top drawer. A smile formed at the perfectly folded socks in order by color. Eric had always been a stickler for order, something they certainly hadn't had in common. Half the time, Izz couldn't even find her socks.

"It's all about organization, Izz," she said in a voice that mocked his. "Start off the morning right, and your whole day will go well." Then she laughed, remembering those playful arguments so well. Good times were had despite their differences.

Her laugh stopped abruptly when her phone beeped. Dread filled her. She hoped it was Cade, perhaps getting up early for work and telling her good morning, but knew deep down who it would be. When she saw the blocked number, she knew she was right.

Mourning period is over, Isabella.

Giving in, Izz decided to just let it all play out. Bring it to an end as Olivia wanted her to do. *What do you want now?*

For history to repeat itself.

She could only guess at what that meant – one of them, her or Cade, or maybe even both, six feet under. Or, perhaps, one of her friends. *What does that even mean?*

Since you insist on staying with your knight in shining armor, the game has changed.

Izz had no idea what the game was to begin with. *So what's your next move?*

Ending you both. Fear for Cade rushed through her and she almost called him, but another message came through. *Tonight, you're safe. Tomorrow, you're safe. When you return, that will change.*

What do you want me to do? Izz waited impatiently, hands shaking slightly.

Return to your dear sweet knight.

Confused, Izz quickly typed out a response. *First you*

tell me to leave him, now you tell me to return? Are you fucking with me or did you forget your own game?

It only took a few seconds for a response. *The game is always changing, dear Isabella. Return to Cade and face your fate.*

And if I don't? If I break it off with him and choose to stay?

If you don't return, dear Isabella, you will find him in pieces.

There was nothing she could do; she realized that now. If she ended her relationship, they were in danger. If she returned to South Carolina, they were in danger. If she called the police and tried to get them both protected, there would always be one moment when evil slipped through the cracks to end their lives. She didn't have a choice. Doing the opposite of what her stalker demanded resulted in Miley's death. This time, she had to listen. She had to return, wait for the next move, and do her damnedest to stay alive.

Overwhelmed with the knowledge of what she was being asked to do, Izz allowed herself to finally break down, for this night only. In the middle of her bedroom floor, knees drawn up to her chest, she cried hot, burning tears until all that was left was the single raging desire to destroy anything that stood in her way.

MYRTLE BEACH WELCOMED HER HOME, an old friend comforting her in the midst of turmoil. Salt in the air beckoned her closer to the crested waves. She drove on autopilot to the house she'd come to think of as her own, especially now that hers was officially on the market.

On my way, she texted Cade. He'd wanted to pick her up from the airport, but she insisted he go to work. He'd missed enough work because of her already, and it was peak tourist season. *Quest* needed him more than she did. He knew to watch his back. She'd learned her lesson before and told him of the messages, but they both knew all they could do now was wait, and attempt some semblance of normal life until then. It may not have been the smartest option, but it was the best one they had.

The roads were fairly clear for a weekday, getting her home much sooner than anticipated. Izz took advantage of the time to start unpacking some of the boxes that had already been delivered in her absence. The week she'd taken in California had given her time to put a rush on some parts of her life, while taking moments of leisure with others. She and Olivia had enjoyed several lunches and dinners, reminiscing over the past, making promises for the future. Together with the twins and Deanna they walked on the beach, hit up a couple local bars like the old days, and spent as much time laughing as possible.

Miley would have wanted them to be happy.

Though it still weighed on her that Miley's case was unresolved and that a deadly unknown awaited her on the east coast, Izz forced on that happy front. She didn't tell her friends about the threatening texts that continued to come through. That, she would deal with when she wasn't in their presence. They had been through enough without having to add all her shit on top of it.

Izz wasn't sure how much of Cade's life she could re-arrange in his home, so she refrained from moving or re-placing too many things. After all, they hadn't even dis-cussed their living arrangements now that she was selling her house. Would she be welcome to stay? Should she get an apartment?

Deep down she knew the answer, but some part of her still felt it was wrong to move this fast with a man she'd known for only a couple months.

Day passed into evening, Izz losing track of time until her rumbling stomach forced her to look at the clock. It was half past eleven, unusually late for Cade to be out, especially knowing she was back in town. With a frown, Izz sent him a quick text, ignoring the worry pricking at the back of her neck.

Are you on your way home? Her fingers hesitated over the word *home*, but she sent the message through an-yway.

No, he isn't.

It took a moment for the response to register, and

when it did, the phone fell from Izz's hand. Her gut churned, heart beating ten times too fast, fear shortening her breath. She forced her body to collect itself as she retrieved the phone.

What do you want? It took her four times to type out the reply with trembling fingers.

Just you.

Where? She held her breath while she waited, feeling her fear slowly fade into something far deadlier.

To the place where it all began. You have twenty minutes. Need I remind you what happens if anyone else shows up?

Izz understood the threat, the same cliché threat she'd written so many times. No cops, just her, wading into the battleground blindfolded and alone. And yet, she knew the power behind that cliché, the truth in the words.

I'll be there.

IT WOULD TAKE TEN MINUTES to get to the place where it all began – *Quest for Avalon*. That was where Cade and Izz first met, where she agreed on one date to get her friends off her back, where it would all come to an end if she didn't pull her shit together.

So, she had ten minutes to figure out what to do.

One of those minutes was spent standing perfectly still while her mind raced into action. Sixty seconds worth of battle plans, *Quest* layouts, and different ways she could either live or die.

Two more minutes had her swiftly changing into a pair of loose black cargo pants, a blank tank top that left her arms free to move, and black boots that laced up her ankles.

One minute later she was racing downstairs while throwing her hair up into a high ponytail, keeping the blonde locks out of her face.

She took three minutes to bound into the living room, pull her sword out from under the couch – she'd never actually gotten around to hanging it after finding the secret box – and slide it in its sheath. Two smaller daggers she took from their cases on a display table and stuck them in the belt at her back. She didn't know if Cade had a gun, let alone where it was, so her weapon of choice would be those of her ancestors.

Two minutes later her sword was in the backseat of her rental car. She leapt in the driver's side and jammed the key in the ignition, impatient with the few seconds it took for the engine to roar to life.

With one minute to spare, Izz collected her thoughts, hands gripping the wheel until her knuckles turned white, eyes focused on the garage door in front of her but not seeing anything except a red haze of rage. She forced her stomach to stop churning and her heart to resume its normal pace, and forced the images of Cade hurt – or worse – out of her thoughts.

Out of time, Izz peeled out of the driveway and sped toward *Quest*.

Chapter
34.

THIS WAS IT, THE MOMENT every message had been leading up to, and she had but mere seconds to formulate a plan. The building was dark when she pulled into a side street and parked, glancing across the road. Izz had never seen *Quest* without all its lights and glamour. It looked eerie in the night, shadowed in dark threats that had her by the throat. But she didn't have time to extract those fingers from around her neck.

She had to go in and cut the damned hand off entirely.

Sliding out of the car and closing the door as quietly as possible, Izz retrieved her weapon from the backseat. She strapped the sheath to her chest and shoulders so the sword rested across her back. The knives she made sure were positioned in her belt so she could easily grab them. The rest was up to her.

As she began the jog across the street, Izz wondered what she must look like to anyone who may happen to see. A woman dressed in black with a weapon strapped to her, clearly up to no good. Somewhere on the surface in that part of her that didn't believe in fantasy, she felt ridiculous and chastised herself for not just calling the police. But, deep down, in the part that longed for a connection that traced back generations, she was eager to play the part of the warrior and see how it all ended using the tools gifted to her by generations of history.

From her pocket, her phone buzzed. Izz spared a moment's glance to see Olivia's name across the screen, and sent the call to voicemail. She didn't have time for friends right now. The buzzing continued as she made her way to the employee entrance in the back, finally stopping by the time she'd opened the door and stepped inside to the darkness that awaited her.

Nerves struck her then, nerves that Izz forced back with a deep breath and shake of her shoulders. The building was quiet, only the sound of horses from the stables to her right meeting her ears. A few dim overhead lights lit her path, casting everything in shadows that reached for her as she slid by, passing the locker rooms, the empty sparring pit, the locked weapons room. Carefully she continued creeping forward, keeping to the walls, eyes scanning every possible hiding place. All the while, she wished she knew exactly what, and who, she was looking for.

A flash of red light caught her eye, a flicker from behind the curtain that led to the arena. Dread filled Izz as she realized exactly where she was about to go, and what she might find on the other side. Her footsteps slowed as she approached, one hand curled around the hilt of a dagger, the other sliding back the curtain. The blood drained from her face when she saw what was behind the cloth.

The chains usually coiled around the wall sides and reserved for the villains of the show were taut, yanked tight toward the center of the arena. And wrapped in them was Cade, bare-chested with his arms outstretched, wrist shackled, head hanging down as his body rested on his knees. Even from the distance she could see the blood on his face and forearms.

"Holy shit," Izz muttered, abandoning caution and racing across the sand to Cade, who appeared to be unconscious. She fell to her knees, sliding into him, and lifted his head, lips pressing together in concern when she saw the gigantic knot on his right temple and the duct tape across his mouth. His torso was bruised, but that could have been from an earlier sparring session. She didn't see any other wounds, except for the lesions at his wrists. Frantically, Izz grabbed at the shackles, but they were locked, and she couldn't loosen the chains to give his arms some slack.

"Cade?" she whispered, lightly tapping his cheek and glancing around to make sure they were alone. The silence was suspicious, but she had other concerns at the moment. "Hey, wake up."

After a few torturous seconds, his eyes opened slowly. When he saw her, Cade jerked, surprised and alarmed by her presence. He shook his head and said something against the tape. "I … I don't understand you. Hold on, this will probably hurt," Izz replied, taking the corner of the tape between her fingers and yanking as fast as she could. The tape peeled off his face to the sound of him cursing. "Sorry. I'm sorry, really." Though she couldn't help the grin that flashed across her face before somberness set in again. "How the hell did you get here?"

"Sucker punch," Cade answered, his quiet reply thick with pain. "Cleaning out the horse stalls." He winced as he tried to readjust and the chains only pulled his arms and shoulders farther apart. "That bitch hit me with a jousting lance."

"That bitch?" Izz repeated.

"Oh yes," a woman's voice said from behind before she could ask for clarification. "That bitch."

She knew that voice, but her brain refused to believe it, until its owner stepped out of the shadows and into view.

"Oh ... you can't be fucking serious." The words escaped Izz's clenched jaw with a mix of incredulousness, confusion, and fury. "How ... Why?"

"How? An entire decade of pretending to be your friend, putting up with all your completely idiotic bullshit until the moment was right. Why? Because just like you, dear Isabella, we all have a destiny to fulfill."

"I trusted you," Izz whispered, turning away from Cade to face the friend she'd mistaken as true. "Deanna ... how could you?"

But the woman before her wasn't Deanna. This was a stranger, looking at her as though they'd never shared a laugh, a tender moment.

"You trusted a lie." Deanna stepped forward, a snarl spreading across her face. "You always thought you were so smart. Fancy writer in a big house, growing up with stories Daddy told you so you'd go to sleep, never actually believing any of it could be real. Thinking yourself so invincible that you never even bothered to look around you."

"You killed Miley." Izz couldn't even process Deanna's other words. Years of deception, Cade in chains behind her, none of it mattered except for that one foremost fact. "You just ... killed her, for what? To send me a message?"

"You weren't getting it, Izz! Ignoring my messages,

moving here to be with your *true love*," she spit out the words like acid. "Something had to be done. Miley annoyed me the most with that obnoxious voice that just grated in your head. She had to go, and had to go first."

"The first?" Frantically, Izz wondered just what Olivia had been calling about so few minutes ago, just as her brain started to put together the pieces. In a flash she remembered meeting Deanna as a drunk coed at a frat party, the way they instantly got along like sisters, Deanna's reservations when she married Eric, her insistence that she stay away from Cade.

"But ... None of this makes sense, Deanna. You wanted me to stay away from him, then you told me to come back. You tell me to return to California, then demand I leave. How the hell is anyone supposed to know what you want if you're so *goddamn schizophrenic*!"

Her shout echoed around the arena, accented by the swoosh of metal in the air as her arm flicked impatiently.

Deanna only shook her head with the smallest of smiles. "Don't you remember the stories, Izz? The trinket that holds all the memories of a lost love, the sword that gives strength and bravery to the knight who fights for good. Such simple objects by themselves, but together holding the power to reunite history with present. Two will live happily ever after, or one will live in the glory of darkness. Either way, someone must die, whether the pieces are reunited or destroyed. I knew you had the sword, and once you found him," she pointed to Cade, "I knew where to find the box. I couldn't have you two figuring it out before I had the chance to stop you, even though this one already knew."

Frustrated, Izz had to restrain herself from simply

lashing out, especially when Deanna shifted and her shirt collar inched to the right just enough to see the edges of a red stone at the hollow of her throat. She needed answers more than bloodshed. "Then why am I here now? Why the theatrics?" Her arms swung out to gesture to the ridiculousness around them.

"Because it entertains me. And because I realized something," Deanna answered as she started to edge her way closer. "That evil you are so afraid of, he wanted the maiden for himself. To own her body, to consume her. But what would I do with you? No, all I want is to live. To make sure destiny never catches up with me. To destroy you both, finish what he started, and end your line for good."

"My line already ends with me, you idiot. You know I can't have kids."

Deanna shook her head. "Destiny, my friend," was all she said, and before Izz could question her, she continued. "Now, let's end this."

When the woman's eyes narrowed in a promise of what was to come, Izz struggled to keep her talking, not yet ready to engage in combat with someone who had meant so much to her. "The knight from *Quest* you said you liked. He was feeding you information."

"And the moron didn't even know it." Deanna took a few steps closer, her tight white shirt reflecting the yellow and red lights flashing around them. Her eyes drifted to Cade. "How easy you men are, sharing all your secrets as soon as a woman shows you any bit of attention."

"Don't talk to him," Izz growled, moving so she stood in front of Cade. "Your business is with me, not him."

Deanna laughed, a sickening sound Izz had never heard before. "Oh, Isabella, my business is with both of you." That wicked laugh sounded again when she moved closer, forcing Izz to lift her hand and point the knife gripped in her fingers in Deanna's direction. "Look at you, Izz, always bringing a knife to gunfight."

With that she revealed her own weapon, a flash of silver that Izz quickly realized was pointed directly at her heart. Instinct kicked in and she leapt to the side, forcing Deanna away from Cade while at the same time spinning, her leg lashing out and connecting with Deanna's arm. The gun dropped to the sand.

"My daddy did more than tell me stories," she said as Deanna held her injured wrist, though the injury didn't stop her from retrieving the weapon. "He taught me how to defend myself and those I love."

"Did he teach you how to save him?" Deanna pointed at Cade, who was fighting against the chains for freedom. The key to his bonds, Izz guessed, was likely somewhere on her former friend's body. "How the tides have turned over the course of history. Rather familiar, wouldn't you say? And we all know how this story ends."

"We write our own destiny." With that, Izz launched into battle.

Chapter 35

THE SOUND OF THREE CONSECUTIVE gunshots blasted through the arena. Where the bullets landed, Izz didn't take the time to find out, knowing only that they didn't hit her or Cade as she spun to avoid the death wounds. Years of practice with her father kicked in and she stabbed at Deanna, who leapt back, finger still poised on the trigger. Before she could make the next shot, Izz sliced downward with the dagger, connecting with flesh. Deanna dropped the gun with a cry and Izz kicked it away, launching it somewhere across the arena.

With a glare worthy of her malicious ancestor, Deanna left her wound to bleed and charged, tackling Izz to the sand. The dagger slipped from her grip the moment her head connected with the ground, dazing her for a few precious seconds. Those seconds were all Deanna needed to land a solid punch to her jaw.

Reacting as quickly as she could, Izz spun beneath Deanna and knocked her off, scrambling to her feet. Deanna turned for the wall and grabbed a battle ax from its hooks. She swung it in front of her, grinning at the look of surprise on Izz's face. "You're not the only one who learned how to fight," she snarled just as she advanced.

The whizz of sharp metal sliced the air next to Izz's head, grazing the tip of her ear. The pain barely had time to register before she went on the offense, reaching back and pulling her sword from its sheath. Though the hilt wasn't a perfect fit, the weight was familiar, its feel giving her strength. Positioning the sword in front of her, Izz readied herself for the fight.

Deanna moved first, side stepping and swinging the ax. Izz blocked the attack, metal screeching against metal as the blades sliced against one another, her arm forced down by the power of the upward attack. Ducking, she dodged the next swing that went just over her head and rolled, at the same time twisting her body so that her sword cut across Deanna's leg. The other woman toppled with a shout of pain as the blade cut through her jeans and into her shin. Thick blood dripped from the wound, but it didn't stop her.

Izz grit her teeth together, both hands holding the sword, her arms already wavering. This wasn't like sparring, when an injury meant a brief pause and weapons were generally less dangerous. Her muscles were burning, her face ached from Deanna's solid right hook, and she was starting to think that one of those bullets found their mark after all, given the sharp, stinging pain in her hip.

The thought made her stumble. With a grin, Deanna threw the ax to the side and yanked a sword from the wall, eyes noting her opponent's injuries. But Izz did the same, seeing the blood still dripping from her wrist, the slight limp in her left leg. Instinct took over and she surged forward to end this war once and for all.

Sword clanged against sword, sparks showering down

on them as they danced across the sand in a series of practiced steps that sent sand flying. It coated their wounds as they tumbled to avoid stabs, leapt to sidestep a swing, fell backward against the force of a kick to the knee.

Watching Deanna closely, Izz anticipated her next move and lashed out with the arm ending in a weapon, connecting with the other blade and twisting her wrist until the sword was wrenched out of her enemy's hand. The blade soared out of reach and Izz pointed her own at Deanna.

"One chance to surrender, D."

"Have at it," Deanna rasped. The only item in reach was a shield, which she plucked from the wall and threw at Izz. Not expecting it, Izz lifted her hands to avoid taking the solid metal to the face, the air forced from her lungs when something barreled into her.

Both women fell to the ground, swords lost, the only weapons their fists. Across the sand they tumbled, Izz landing hard blows to Deanna's stomach and face until Deanna managed to grab a fistful of hair. Izz's head was forced back and her body followed until she wasn't sure which way was up. All she knew was the agony shooting fire though her blood.

She knew she had to get away, to take a moment to recoup. Working her leg up, Izz kicked Deanna solidly in the chest. They both fell at the move and scrambled away from one another, two bruised and bloody masses of torn clothing and shredded skin.

Exhausted, Izz fell back against the wall. Across the arena, Deanna did the same. They stared at one another, chests heaving, eyes narrowed in anticipation. Both wanted to fight but neither had the energy yet to move.

Izz took advantage of the break to access her injuries. Her face ached and she tasted blood. There was a dull pain in her stomach from Deanna's fists that clenched when she breathed. Her hip felt like it was on fire, and one touch brought her fingers back covered in dark-red blood. And after taking a boot to the knee, she wasn't entirely sure she could walk.

But they were flesh wounds, mostly. A little blood and pain wouldn't stop her from doing what needed to be done, even if that meant killing her former friend. Just like that, years of friendship and love were severed from her consciousness. All that mattered now was saving Cade and destroying anyone in her path.

After a moment, Deanna broke the silence, her words breathy. "You can't save him, Isabella. Or yourself. It's destiny. Death has followed you since the moment you were born."

Izz's parents' death flashed before her eyes, followed by Eric's. His passing made her breath catch. "Did you kill Eric, D?"

Deanna huffed, shaking her head once. "Why would I kill Eric? He was the only one standing between you and your knight in shining armor. *You* killed Eric, by letting yourself love someone you weren't meant to love."

The guilt she'd tried so hard to force away washed back up, stinging her heart and soul. Deep down she'd always known it was somehow her fault. The way they never quite clicked, the hesitation she'd felt on their wedding day, the feeling that both of them were simply settling. It wasn't hard to love Eric, and love him she did, but even now Izz could admit it wasn't the kind of passion that transcended history. It had been comfortable.

It had been his death sentence.

"Don't listen to her, Isabella," Cade's voice broke through. He could read the pain on her face, and worried what it would mean in this moment on the battlefield.

Deanna pushed herself to her feet with a grunt, stalking over to him and forcing his head up by his hair. "Don't get cute, loverboy." With a chuckle, she lowered herself to his level. "You know, when Olivia suggested getting you to charm our dear friend Isabella, I'd hoped you were the one I was waiting for. The timing was so perfect. All I had to do was let it all play out. You made my job so much easier."

If she was planning to say anything else, Izz wasn't sure, because at that moment Cade reared back and slammed his forehead into her nose. Even from a distance, Izz heard the crunch and took dark satisfaction in it.

Before Deanna could recover, Cade leapt up and wrapped his legs around her waist, her body twisting to the side as he slammed her to the sand. The movement caused his arms to jerk and a sickening popping sounded just as he clenched his jaw and bit back a rough groan of pain.

But he didn't let go.

He felt something tear in his shoulder, the searing pain only fueling the strength in his legs as he held Deanna captive, squeezing until the air choked out of her in almost sobbing gasps. Her hands searched the sand frantically for a weapon, and he saw a second too late the small knife she managed to grasp and send directly into his thigh.

Cade's legs dropped as he let loose a roar mixed with fury and fire, arms yanking against the chains in a way that had him hanging awkwardly, trying not to further injure his dislocated shoulder. In front of him, Deanna fell to her stomach, rising to her hands and knees shakily. Through the red haze, Cade managed to lift his good leg and kick her squarely in the ribs.

The force of the hit, one that he knew must have cracked a few bones, sent her stumbling back, retreating. Izz took the opportunity to dart back to Cade with a frantic half-crawl and search for a way to free him of his chains. Her fingers slipped on the blood coating his wrists. Through wide eyes she saw the way the metal was cutting into flesh.

She knew it was useless. No amount of tugging or cursing would break the chains unless she had the key. But even knowing that didn't stop her from trying, desperate to help him, to heal that look of agony written in his expression.

"Isabella!"

Deanna's shout had Izz spinning around. The woman had risen to her feet, one hand wrapped around her midsection, the other holding a knife. Torn between charging forward in attack and turning behind to free her love, Izz stalled in place, her mind frantically working through different options until it reached its conclusion.

In front of her, Deanna sneered. Behind her, Cade said her name quietly. When she turned he saw the decision lighting a fire in her eyes.

"It's okay," he said quietly, before she could say anything.

Risking the move, Izz dropped to her good knee and put her hands on either side of Cade's face, seeing his attention glance over his shoulder. He would be her eyes in this moment. "I can't get you out," she whispered, her voice almost a sob. "I have to get the key from her. I … I have to do this fight on my own."

"It's okay," Cade repeated, appearing exhausted but oddly comfortable with the thought of her taking over, as though she hadn't been doing that all along.

"But you're hurt."

He shook his head against her protest. "I'm alive. You're alive. Write your own destiny." His eyes almost sparkled when he added, "Tonight, you be the knight, and I'll be your damsel."

Tears pricked the corners of her eyes as Izz laughed, finding his reply so charming and absurd that it was easy to forget her pain for just one moment. He gave her a smile that strengthened her and she rose to her feet. Sword in hand, Izz advanced, Deanna readying herself only a few feet away.

"This is it, D." Izz tried to hide her limp, just as Deanna attempted to hide her weakening arm and ribs. "No more breaks. No more words. We fight until one of us is dead."

"About time," was all Deanna said before she swung out.

The arena disappeared as Izz turned all her focus on woman and weapon. The lights centered on her enemy, all sound transformed into nothing but metal and air, her sight tunneled into a line of fire. In that moment Izz channeled the knight Cade knew she could be, hundreds of battles and thousands of years of skill backing her every move.

But Deanna knew the skill she faced, and matched it almost just as evenly. Her eyes flashed as she lifted her arm to block an attack, then used her own momentum to shove Izz away, both of them losing their weapons, unable to hold on in their exhaustion.

Deanna grabbed Izz around her wrists, just as Izz took hold of her by the throat. Locked together, the pair stumbled into the wall, lances tumbling down on top of them, but their grips never faltered. They rose to their feet in unison, Izz tightening her hold, Deanna prying her fingers away with one hand while fisting a hand in her shirt with the other.

With a single hard jerk, Deanna yanked Izz against her and slammed her forehead down. Izz dropped to the sand, not entirely convinced she hadn't blacked out for a moment when she looked up through blurry vision to see Deanna stumbling away from her. She could vaguely hear her former friend saying something to Cade as she leaned down on shaky legs to retrieve something. The gun, Izz realized when she saw the shiny metal.

Terror urged her to her knees. Her foot clunked against something hard, and Izz nearly gasped in relief at the sight of her sword. She pulled it in front of her, at the same time realizing she had something in the hand that had been wrapped around Deanna's throat.

The red stone on a black lace chain stared up at her, the trinket from the box hidden in Cade's wall. Next to the stone was a key. Izz could only stare at the necklace for the briefest of moments, frowning when she made to close her fist around it only to have the stone fall from its setting. She retrieved it from the sand, looking between it and Deanna, who was making her way to Cade, too far away to reach by blade alone.

Izz fell back on her knees, trying to get up but her body betraying her will as her legs gave out and her head swam with blurry visions. Tears formed as she watched Deanna's approach, seeing Cade fighting to stand on his good leg, make some attempt at self-defense. She was still talking to Cade as her arm lifted, gun pointed at the center of his forehead.

The stone in her hand suddenly felt ten times its weight and Izz glanced down. Something about the shape of the jewel out of its setting felt familiar, and in the haze clouding her mind an idea brewed.

With a trembling hand, Izz brought the red stone to the sword, hovering it over the indentation in the gold she'd always wondered about. As if it had been waiting for the piece to complete it.

For good to triumph, the two pieces of the prophecy must be reunited. Bits of the story floated back at her, a story staring her straight in the face, daring her to believe.

Izz dropped the stone in its new setting and pressed down lightly, a perfect fit. Something in the hilt shifted beneath her hand. There was a click as she pressed down, a latch catching, and when the long blade shook ever so slightly, she suddenly knew all the secrets this sword held.

"Look at you, Izz," she whispered as she lifted her arm in one final burst of strength, thumb poised over the red stone, "always bringing a knife to a gunfight."

Cade, eyes trained on the gun mere inches from his head, didn't see the moment her thumb pressed down. He didn't see the chain reaction that single, simple movement caused, so focused was he on the furious woman in front of him with a bloody and crooked nose and vengeful glare. But from his vantage point, he did see the blade of the sword cut its way through Deanna's chest.

He could only stare in wonder as the woman dropped the gun, shock and pain radiating across her face, blood quickly staining the white of her shirt. She dropped to her knees, then to her side, unable to speak, only able to gasp for air that curdled in her lungs.

Izz picked herself up off the sand and hobbled over. Seeing Deanna dying in front of her took her breath away, her heart breaking for the woman she'd loved even as it celebrated the end of her enemy. The conflict hurt almost as much as her other injuries … but not enough to save her.

Leaning over so that only Deanna could hear her words, Izz whispered, "Welcome to the other end of a sucker punch."

Deanna stared up at her, eyes wide, mouth moving but no words coming out. Izz ignored her attempts to speak and pushed away. Knowing she no longer had anything to worry about, she turned her back on Deanna and quickly unlocked the cuffs from around Cade's wrists. Cade fell against her, catching himself after shifting his weight to his uninjured leg. He wrapped his good arm around Izz and pulled her a few feet away from Deanna.

They watched, together, as the life drained out of her.

Chapter 36

WHEN IT WAS OVER, FINALLY, blessedly, over, Izz allowed herself a moment to turn her head into Cade's shoulder. Though she forced back the tears, she couldn't help the few sniffles that escaped.

"Still want me to move in?" she asked, needing to speak, to hear his voice. "Apparently I'm high risk."

Cade smiled against her hair. "Apparently you know how to kick ass. I think I'm safe with you, m'lady." He shifted then, pulling the hilt of the sword out of her hand. "Care to explain this?"

Izz pointed to the stone. "I figured it out, why the two pieces had to come together. It wasn't for some grand magical purpose, but a rather simple fighting technique. Clever, really." She pushed on the stone and Cade heard the reaction inside, some sort of spring-loaded mechanism that had dislodged the blade from the hilt with enough force to put it through a person's body. Normally he wouldn't have believed it to be true, but then, they had just settled a vendetta thousands of years old.

Right now, anything was possible.

"Maybe this is a good time to tell you that I didn't tell

you the whole truth." Cade lifted a brow when Izz turned her head to stare up at him suspiciously. "In the story your father always told you, of the knight and the maiden. I'm not a descendant of the knight."

Her mouth twisted into a frown. "Then who is?" When realization set in, Izz shook her head. "No. You said our tattoos were some long-lost desire for one another, so we would recognize each other."

"I said no such thing. You did, and I merely let you assume that."

She struggled to think back to what he'd said about his markings. *"It's a symbol from my family's past. A reminder of where we came from, to always be brave, to remember the ones we fight for, and to be prepared for the trials we face in the future."*

"But … Then why did you have the box, and I had the sword?"

"Because one of the stories got it right. The maiden's family stole the box and gave away the sword. What they don't say is that they gave the sword to the knight's grandson, in hopes that if the magic was true after all, the two would find their way back to one another without evil getting in the way."

"How do you know all this?"

Cade gave a one-shouldered shrug. "My family knew its history, and knew it well. We even traced the other sides, but got lost the closer to present day. We tried to find you, and find *her*." He gestured to the body bleeding out in the sand. "But the lines got blurry, and eventually we couldn't see them at all."

"So Deanna never knew," Izz surmised. "She thought, like me, it was the other way around. Why didn't you tell me?"

"Because you needed to find your courage outside of a story, Isabella. And, it's more entertaining for me watching you figure it all out."

Izz laughed then, a full laugh that had him smiling as well. "You sneaky son of a bitch." She kissed him hard, not even caring that yet another piece of truth had been kept from her. And it was that hidden truth that had her pulling back. She looked up into Cade's dark eyes with a single brow lifted. "So, basically, what you're telling me is that all along, you were just a lonely maiden waiting for your knight in shining armor?"

The teasing in her voice had him taking a firm grip on her hair, tipping her head back until his mouth claimed hers. The force of the kiss had her melting against him, nearly groaning in frustration when he pulled away.

Smooth, too smooth. The mantra repeated in her head like a long-running joke.

"I do believe my sword is bigger than yours, m'lady."

"Perv." Izz shoved him and stood, finally taking in the somber scene around her that she wasn't really ready to face, but had to finish. The harsh reality of Deanna's death overshadowed the otherwise tender moment. It was time to call the police, and deal with whatever came next.

Together, finally, as one.

Epilogue

THEY WATCHED THE SHOW FROM the back wall, slipping out before the tournament began, Cade casting a final glance over his shoulder before he left the show behind for a while. He'd always be the owner of *Quest for Avalon*, but his time performing as a knight fighting for the maiden's hand in marriage had come to an end.

He'd found the one he'd been searching for. The one he'd been fighting for.

Taking her hand in his, Cade led Izz onto the beach, the place where he felt their connection truly began. She walked beside him silently. Both of them contemplated the past month, how long it had taken for everything to get sorted with the police, in California, in South Carolina.

Once they had a person to fit the crime, it hadn't been hard for the police to find the evidence they needed. Deanna had kept a lot from everyone over the years, more than Izz had ever imagined, more than anyone could have ever predicted. The amount of information Deanna had saved in secret computer files and tucked away in her safe on Izz and her family shocked them all, though not as much as the family tree tracing her lineage as far back as the origins of the prophecy.

Izz lost track of how many times she felt blindsided by new facts coming to the surface. Though, the final blow had come when she finally found out why Olivia had been so frantically calling her the night it all came to an end. The unannounced visit she'd made to Deanna's apartment, the neighbor who informed her of the woman leaving in the middle of the night with a single piece of luggage, and the suspicion that led Olivia to sifting through the trash only to find a single receipt for a pair of rubber cleaning gloves and bleach. While on the surface it didn't appear like much, her gut had told her to dig deeper, and the police did the rest.

With the investigation closed, their lives returned to a state of normalcy they'd come to accept. Olivia still hadn't recovered from stumbling upon one of her best friends dead in a closet, but was starting to sleep better again at night. The twins went back to their families, with Beth expecting a new addition in the coming months. And Izz, she finally let herself love again.

At times she still felt guilty over Eric's death, perhaps even more so by Miley's, and on those nights Cade held her close, whispering words of comfort as she cried herself to sleep. She'd come to accept the role that fate played in all of their lives, but it didn't make it easier to let go of the pains buried deep in her heart – pains over her role in the death of two people she loved dearly, pains over the loss of a friend turned enemy, pains over the fact that she could never return to her old life. When her house sold, those aches lessened some, as though she was given permission to move on somewhere new, with someone new.

With those thoughts in mind, Izz shifted closer to

Cade, enjoying the feel of his warmth so close to her. The arm around her shoulder tightened and she nestled into him, both of them careful to avoid their respective injuries still healing even weeks after the final battle in the arena. Cade's arm was out of the sling but still tender, her knee remained wrapped in a brace, and bruises marred their flesh. But none of it mattered when they were next to one another.

The moment was interrupted by her phone buzzing in her pocket. A flash of dread speared her gut before she told herself that Deanna was dead. The days of threatening messages were over.

I miss you, girl.

Izz smiled at Olivia's text, missing her friend just as much. It was hard, being on opposite ends of the country, and already she was planning on ways to get her friend to move to the east coast.

You miss borrowing my clothes, she replied, knowing it was at least partly true.

Busted, was the answer. Then after a few seconds, *Knight-Maiden being good to you?*

Olivia had taken to calling Cade by the new moniker, much to Izz's amusement and Cade's chagrin. *Same old knight in shining armor.*

Good. So ... California misses you too. Are you ever coming back?

A grin worked its way over her face as she realized there was only one reply to give her friend. Izz quickly typed out the words, then, in a moment of pure abandonment, chucked the phone somewhere in the sand and grabbed hold of Cade. She tugged him closer to the shore, and together they bounded into the waves, laughing, wrapped up in one another, all while her answer to Olivia rang in her thoughts.

Not today, Liv. I've got a man to get under.

Want more of Riley, Rowan, and medieval knights?

Don't miss these companion novels hitting shelves 2015!

Dawn Pendleton – *Riley*
Jordan Deen – *Beyond the Emerald Knight*
Amy Miles - *TBA*

OTHER TITLES TO CHECK OUT
BY KRISTINA CIRCELLI

The Whisper Legacy
Beyond the Western Sun
Walk the Red Road
Into the Shadow Realm

Standalone Novels
The Never
Fragile Creatures
The Sour Orange Derby
Fade into the Woodwork
A Single Swim

The Helping Hands Series
The Helping Hands
Shadows in the Night
The Iron Fist
Abandon

Acknowledgments

A BIG THANK YOU TO everyone who continues to support me in this crazy writer dream!

For my family: Your unwavering encouragement and belief in my goals keep me going. Y'all are my biggest fans and best marketers.

For my readers: Y'all make it all possible! I love having the opportunity to share my words with every one of you.

For Kristi and Sam: I love being able to talk to you about books and life in general. We may not see each other often (okay, or ever) in person, but I consider you two of my closest friends.

For Juli: My favorite editor! I'm so honored to have an editor who is also a friend that "gets it."

For Julie: My favorite formatter! You are so seriously skilled in what you do that I have no words. Just stares of awe.

For Dawn, Jordan, and Amy: Who would have thought that an innocent writers' retreat would result in a tradition of knights? I'm so lucky to be friends with three awesome maidens such as yourselves.

For Sarah: You do amazing work. Thank you for a fantastic cover, and sorry again it took me so long to realize I had those glasses all along...

For Our Knights: Ryan, David, Casy, and Ripp. Kudos to you for taking four possibly crazy women seriously and humoring us in our venture to put together a book series about knights. We appreciate you taking time out of your busy schedules to join us in the photo shoot! In the words of Ripp Baker, "I don't know about you guys, but I'm having a blast."

Meet the Author

NIGHT OWL, DORITO LOVER, AND quiet eccentric - Kristina Circelli is the author of several fiction novels, including The Helping Hands series, The Whisper Legacy, Fragile Creatures, The Never, and The Sour Orange Derby.

A descendant of the Cherokee nation and fan of all things magic, Circelli holds both a Bachelor of Arts and Master of Arts in English from the University of North Florida, where she teaches creative writing. She also heads Red Road Editing, a full-service editing company for independent authors and commercial clients.

She currently resides in Jacksonville, Florida with her husband, Seth, and cats, Lord Finnegin the Fierce and Master Malachi the Mighty.

Connect with Kristina

FACEBOOK
https://www.facebook.com/authorkristinacircelli

TWITTER
https://twitter.com/kcircelli

WEBSITE
http://www.circelli.info/

BLOG
http://anawfullybigadventure-kc.blogspot.com/

www.ingramcontent.com/pod-product-compliance
Lightning Source LLC
Chambersburg PA
CBHW022154170626
46807CB00005B/2208